Loving MAN

BAILEY WEST

LOVING MAN

BAILEY WEST

SYNOPSIS

The week of the culinary conference was Xander Northcott's time to shine. Fresh out of a long-term relationship, he cemented his newly single status by accepting Piper Andrews's invitation back to her room that first night. It was all fun and games until a few months later, when he received a phone call from the woman he barely knew.

She was pregnant—with his child.

Heralded as a culinary savant, Angel Saint Rose studied alongside the world's best Chocolatiers. It wasn't just a job for her. When honing her skills with chocolate confections, she was in her element—until she received a phone call that changed her life.

And killed her passion.

When Xander and Angel's roads converge, can they call on each other to help find their way back?

Xander

"Mr. Northcott, you can put the stroller at the top of the jet bridge, and someone will put it under the plane for you," the airline gate agent said after putting a pink tag on the stroller.

"Do I keep him in the car seat or am I supposed to take him out?"

"Most people hold their infants, but I see you have two seats so you can keep him in it," the gate agent responded.

"Thank you," I said.

I took my tickets back from her and proceeded through the boarding gate. After pushing the stroller to the end of the jet bridge, I located the buttons to pop the car seat off the stroller's top. The clerk at the baby boutique gave me step by step instructions on the stroller at least ten times before I finally figured it out. Not being prepared to get a crash course in baby formula, baby clothes, baby necessities, and baby care all at once, I memorized what I could and took notes for the rest. The last few days had been a whirlwind.

The flight attendant greeted me as I boarded the plane. I found my seat near the front, put the car seat in the window seat, put the diaper bag in the overhead compartment, and sat down with a huff. I looked over at him to make sure all the moving hadn't awakened him. He was still asleep. I was grateful.

He slept soundly while the other passengers filed onto the plane and found their seats. I didn't know how long he would be asleep, but I hoped he would at least allow me to close my eyes for a few minutes. I was utterly exhausted. My fumes were running on fumes. Sleep at night seemed to elude us both. I was afraid I would sleep too hard and not hear him crying. He was a newborn and wasn't expected to sleep at night. I was a new dad, learning how to care for him, and he was learning how to be alive.

"Good morning, ladies and gentlemen. Welcome aboard. Thank you for your attention while important safety information is reviewed," one of the flight attendants said over the speaker.

The announcement seemed louder than usual. I quickly looked over to see if he was still asleep. He was. I let out a sigh of relief and rested my head on the back of the chair. Watching his little chest rise and fall, I marveled at how small and perfect he was.

I hadn't realized that I'd fallen asleep until his whimpering roused me. We'd been flying for about thirty minutes, according to my watch. After I retrieved the diaper bag, I took a bottle of milk from the bag's thermal section to put it into the battery-operated bottle warmer. The bottle warmer was another item the clerk at the baby boutique told me I'd needed and taught me how to use.

His whimpering started to get louder, so I unbuckled him from his seat and picked him up.

"Make sure he feels close to you, Dad." "A light tap on his bottom as you rock him will help calm him." I recalled all the tips and tricks I had learned from the nurses at the hospital.

Maximus and I had just began our journey together as father and son. I met his mother, Piper, nine months ago, while I was in California for a culinary conference. Her beautiful mocha skin, long legs, killer walk, and full lips instantly attracted me to her. So, when she approached me at the hotel bar, it was a no brainer that I purchased her a drink and then invited her to dinner.

She was funny, smart, and worked for one of the vendors at the conference. I wasn't surprised when she told me she was one of the company's top sales representatives. She had almost sold me on a product I didn't even need.

After dinner, she invited me to her room. I wasn't necessarily the type of guy that had spontaneous one-night stands, but I was fresh out of a long-term relationship and I figured why not.

She and I spent the subsequent nights of the conference talking about the food industry, having dinner and sex. We knew it was just a fling. Neither of us was ready to be in anything long-term, but we'd promised to stay in touch.

I was surprised when I'd received a call from her almost two months later informing me that she was pregnant and planned on keeping it. Of course, my first thought was about the baby's paternity since we'd only been together that week and used protection every time except once. Before I could ask the question, she said she'd scheduled a prenatal paternity test. The only thing I needed to do was go to the lab and get my cheek swabbed. The results came back ninety-nine percent positive the baby was mine. We'd discussed the plan to raise the child together, a co-parenting situation. We worked through our lawyers to ensure everything was fair for the baby and us. She kept me updated on the progress of the pregnancy, even FaceTiming me at the doctor visits. I flew back to California twice: once to go to a regular prenatal visit and the other to find out the sex of the baby. After expressing a desire to be there when my son was born, we scheduled an induction at thirty-nine weeks.

Maximus Alexander Northcott came into the world weighing in at six pounds, five ounces. When the nurse placed him in my arms, it felt like my heart had expanded, and in that instant, I knew what unconditional love felt like.

"I will never stop loving you," I'd said as I held him close.

Soon after his birth Maximus and Piper were given a clean bill of health and discharged from the hospital. I'd planned to stay in California the first few days to help Piper get adjusted to caring for a new baby. A day after being discharged from the hospital, she'd complained about severe pain in her stomach. Her doctor told her that it was normal afterbirth pain.

"Something's wrong, Xander. I need to go back to the hospital," Piper said after the second day of abdominal pain.

I'd taken her back to the hospital and they admitted her due to fever and dehydration. Two days later, she'd passed from an infection that, if they would've taken her complaints seriously, could have been treated, and she would've been fine.

She didn't have much family, one aunt that she spoke of. I paid for the small funeral with her aunt and her friends and brought Maximus home with me. While filling out the official paperwork for his birth certificate, I'd changed his middle name from Alexander to Andrew in honor of his mother, Piper Andrews.

Just as the bottle warmer chimed, Maximus' soft whimpers morphed into a high-pitched wail. He had healthy, strong lungs for such a small human. He was hungry and I had taken too long to prepare his food. I rushed to get the bottle to him, but he was too angry to take it.

It felt like his cries said, "You wanted to take your time? Now feel my wrath!"

His little face was contorted into a small red ball of fury with his eyes tightly closed and his toothless mouth opened wide for maximum sound. I was flustered and had no idea what he wanted. I tried again with the bottle. A couple drops of milk dropped from the nipple into his mouth, but the taste of milk did not stop his cry. I was afraid to keep trying with the bottle because I didn't want the milk to cause him to choke. I tried to rock him and shush him – no luck. I tried to stand and walk a little – he wasn't having it. I knew the other people on the plane were not happy with us, but I couldn't even be concerned about their feelings. I needed to figure out how to calm my son down. Having zero exposure to a newborn before him, I didn't have any tricks up my sleeve. I'd almost resolved myself to an awfully long, noisy flight home.

"Excuse me?" I heard come from beside me as I stood in the aisle about to have a tantrum with Maximus.

"Yes?" I answered before I turned to face a beautiful woman with big, bright Disney character eyes and a beautiful smile.

"Can I help you with the baby? Maybe I can get him to calm down?" she offered.

I was aware of stranger danger and crazy people who kidnapped kids. However, I was disarmed by her genuine smile, beautiful eyes, and open arms to receive Maximus.

"Okay," I said and passed him to her.

"Well, hello, beautiful baby," she sweetly sang to Maximus. "You are having a hard time. Is it the pressure on your ears, or did you wake up too early, humph?"

She spoke to him like she intended for him to respond. Then he stopped crying like he was trying to hear what she said.

"Yeah, I know. I hate planes sometimes, too. Can I try the bottle again?" she asked.

"Sure." I quickly passed the bottle to her.

She took the bottle and gave it to Maximus. He hungrily accepted it like I'd never tried it.

Really Maximus?

"Can I sit?" she asked.

"Yes," I hurriedly removed the car seat from Maximus' seat. She sat down and continued to feed him.

"I can put that in her seat if you don't mind?" the flight attendant said.

I nodded my approval.

"Yeah, you were a little gassy, huh?" she continued to speak. "What's his name?"

"Maximus," I responded.

"Maximus," she softly repeated. "Ah, it fits. I'm Angel."

"Xander," I replied. "Nice to meet you."

"Nice to meet both of you. How old is he?" she asked.

"He's almost two weeks."

"You just got here, welcome," she whispered.

Maximus happily drank his bottle like he and I weren't on the verge of being pushed from the plane with parachutes a few moments earlier.

"He's beautiful," she smiled.

"Thank you. I don't know why he got so angry with me."

"He's tooted at least three times over here, so I think he was just a little gassy," she said.

"I'm sorry!"

"Don't be. It's fine. I used to babysit my little cousins. I've experienced much, much worse, believe me."

I rested my head on the seat and watched Maximus drink his bottle and start to doze off. Angel rested her head on the wall and watched him eat. I had no idea how I was going to survive this. I had no child-care plan in place. We were about to open another restaurant location, so work would be hectic. I didn't have the time or know-how to be a father.

I'd reached out to my friend who was a pediatrician and he'd connected me with a nanny referral agency. The agency would send me several candidates to interview for a full-time nanny position. I'd purchased a crib and a changing table. Still, I hadn't put it together because I hadn't planned on Maximus visiting any time soon. Piper and I had agreed that I would visit him in California until he was old enough to travel. I had no idea how I would get everything done that needed to be completed and keep it all together.

"Don't worry, Dad. You will survive," Angel softly said like she was reading my thoughts. "He's only going to be this small for a brief amount of time."

I smiled, hoping she was right.

"Are you from Sable Falls or just visiting?" I asked.

"I'm from California, but I live in Sable. I was out in California visiting with family for a couple months," she explained.

"Back to the grind, huh?"

"Unfortunately," she said.

Maximus looked so content resting in Angel's arms. She handed me the bottle and gently leaned Maximus forward while supporting his neck. She patted his back a couple times before he let out a huge burp.

"Wow, that was a grown man-sized burp," she chuckled.

"That was a belch!" I laughed.

She placed his face on the burp cloth that rested on her shoulder.

"I can take him," I offered.

"No, I can tell you're tired. You can rest. He's fine," she smiled.

I woke up to the pilot's announcement about our final descent. I quickly turned and looked at Maximus. He was still resting in Angel's arms, and she was sleeping.

"Angel," I whispered as I touched her shoulder. "The plane is about to land."

"Wow, I didn't realize I fell asleep," she answered.

"I know, I dozed off, too."

"I guess I better get back to my seat. He's a beautiful baby and is going to be an amazing human. Your legacy will be safe with him," she said as she passed him to me.

"Thank you," was all I could muster. Her words were thoughtful and unexpectedly hit me in an emotional way.

"It was such a pleasure meeting you, Maximus," she whispered to him.

She went back to her seat and returned with Maximus' car seat.

"Thank you," I responded.

"It was my pleasure," she smiled.

"*S*he could've been a real angel."

"A real angel?" I asked Tatiana, my twin sister.

"I mean, you said you didn't see her after the plane landed. You looked for her at the baggage claim and she wasn't there. Maybe she disappeared. You know there are real angels among us."

"I did have to wait for his stroller to be brought to the jet bridge, so I was a little late getting to baggage claim. She could've just gotten her bag and left."

"Or..." Tatiana chuckled.

"Whatever," I laughed. "How is everything going there?"

"It was going great until I got word that my little nephew was born, his mom passed, and my brother doesn't want me to come home to help him."

"Don't do that! You know I want you here, but I don't want you stepping away from the opportunity of a lifetime to come and sit with me. You couldn't bring Piper back and you know nothing about babies, so you would just be in the way."

"I'm great with babies," she responded.

"What babies have you been around?"

"Plenty," her voice cracked.

"Exactly, zero!" I laughed.

"Whatever!" she laughed.

Tatiana was a classically trained violinist. She'd been playing since we were five years old. We'd both started violin lessons, but I quickly realized I didn't want to be a musician. I wanted to be an athlete. While I'd played football, basketball, and baseball, Tati was recognized as a musical prodigy and had traveled around the country with different orchestras.

She'd just started playing with the Vienna Philharmonic in Austria. She'd dreamed of being able to join one of the world's best orchestras. When they sought her out and offered her a position, she quickly accepted and moved to Austria. Their practice season had just begun. There was no way I would've let her leave for me.

"Well, at least put the camera back on him, so I can watch him sleep," Tati said.

I rotated the camera on my phone and focused on him in his crib.

"He is so beautiful. I know this is hard for you, but you are going to survive," Tatiana swooned.

"Angel said the same thing on the plane," I recalled.

"See, I told you. She probably doesn't have a real name since she's an angel, so she just used angel as her name," Tatiana concluded.

"Angels have names," I retorted.

"Name one angel," Tatiana responded.

"Michael, Gabriel, Della Reese. You didn't listen at all in Sunday School."

We both laughed.

Angel had crossed my mind more than once since Maximus and I had arrived home. She seemed so comfortable with Maximus, which made me feel comfortable. I hoped I would find a nanny with her calming ability. I beat myself up for not asking Angel more questions like her last name or what part of town she lived in. She'd made an impact on my life in such a short time.

"I have some interviews for a nanny tomorrow. I thought about daycare, but my schedule is so hectic that I need live-in help."

"Plus, daycares are cesspools," Tati said.

"We went to daycare when Mom started working."

"And look at how we turned out!" Tati laughed.

"Can't argue with that," I laughed.

"Who are these people that you'll be interviewing to take care of my nephew?"

"The nanny agency matched me with them. They sent me all their resumes, and they all look good on paper. Hopefully, someone will work out. I only have another week before I need to be back to work."

"What if you don't like any of the candidates?" Tati asked.

"Then he's coming to work with me or I'm not going. He has to be my number one priority."

"Look at you, sounding like a dad! Who are you and what have you done with my brother?" Tati laughed.

"It's been a hard, few days, Sister," I finally admitted out loud.

I'd been holding it all together, but this whole situation was challenging.

"I know. I can feel your struggle, Brother. Who would've thought you would've been the first one with a kid?"

"Right! As fast as you were in undergrad," I teased.

"Shut up! I was just doing what Mommy told me, having fun before I became an adult," Tati responded.

"And now? You're thirty and still fast."

"Shut up, Xander!" she laughed.

Maximus stirred a little but continued to sleep.

"But for real, I know the circumstances are bad, but I'm glad he's here and I'm glad he's with you. Are you sure you don't want me to come home?"

"Of course I want you to come home, but I don't want you to miss your opportunity. We are going to be here when you get your break."

"What about Mommy and Daddy? Have you been able to reach them yet?" Tati asked.

"They are scheduled to call soon. I didn't want to use the emergency number because, like you, there really isn't anything they can do."

"Mommy is going to try to be on the next thing flying when she finds out."

"I know. Hopefully, I can talk them out of it."

"When have you ever been able to talk Mommy out of anything she put her mind to?" Tati asked.

"Never," I responded.

"Just be prepared for her wrath and probably some tears," Tati said.

I took a deep breath. "I will be prepared."

"Piper is looking down at you and smiling. She found the right one-night stand to knock her up. The one time you finally let go and have some fun and look what happened!" Tati chuckled.

"Shut up. Go and enjoy Austria. I will call you later."

"I will. Hopefully, they won't kick me out of the country for running down the hill singing 'The Hills are Alive', from *The Sound of Music*," she laughed.

"Hopefully, they won't."

"Alright, Brother. I love you."

"Love you too, Sister."

2

Xander

"He's healthy. All his labs look great. You said he's up to three ounces of milk per feeding?" Everett, Maximus's pediatrician, asked.

Everett and his family had moved into our neighborhood the summer of our freshman year of high school. We were introduced through our parents and became best friends. People had friends that they only told parts of their story because they didn't want to be judged, but Everett was the one person that knew my entire life story. He never judged, just listened. He and his wife Kerry had been incredibly supportive through all the recent events. They'd put the nursery together once I knew I would be bringing Maximus home. Everett had also arranged to have Maximus and Piper's medical records sent to him, ensuring that he would have all the information if anything medically related happened in the future. Kerry had gone to the store and purchased clothes and pampers for Maximus. I wouldn't have made it without them.

"Yeah, he's really putting them away. He likes the milk from *Milk Bank,* so thank you for the prescription."

"No problem. There are so many mothers who produce enough milk to feed their babies and donate. Breastmilk is the best for him. I'm glad he likes it. You can get him dressed while I finish filling out his chart. How are you doing?" Everett said.

I started putting Maximus' clothes back on him.

"I'm surviving. Learning something new every day. I had zero knowledge of babies. He's teaching me a lot."

"Has Emmaline been over to see him yet?"

"Nope. She threw a fit when I told her the trip to Dubai had to be canceled because Maximus was coming home with me," I explained.

"A fit? Why? Doesn't she understand the circumstances?" Everett asked.

"She's got her own agenda," I shrugged.

"I swear I don't understand why you are still with her. I thought you would've moved on after y'all broke up. I turn around and she had her claws back in you," Everett shook his head.

Emmaline, my girlfriend, and Everett did not get along. He'd never liked her, but he'd tolerated her because he and I were friends. My long-term relationship with Emmaline had ended right before I met Piper. Emmaline and I had agreed that our relationship had become strained. We'd grown apart and needed space away from each other. After several months of being apart, Emmaline and I started talking again and decided to give the relationship another try. At that point I had to tell her about Piper's pregnancy and our co-parenting plan. After mulling it over, she'd decided she was okay with my impending fatherhood.

Emmaline didn't want children, so her agreeing to the relationship after knowing about my son was a surprise. Her response to my call about Piper's death, however, was not a surprise. She was not thrilled that we had to cancel our trip and that I would now be a full-time father.

"She's comfortable," I shrugged. "We will see how she handles having Maximus around."

"Why did she stick around when you told her about lil' man coming?"

"I don't know. She acted like she was fine with it. I think maybe because we thought I wouldn't have him a lot, but now," I shrugged.

"So, what's the play?"

"I have no idea. Honestly, I haven't put much thought into anything except Maximus."

"Did you get in touch with that nanny agency I recommended?" Everett asked.

"I did. I have four interviews this afternoon. I am meeting them after we leave here."

"Good. You know Kerry and I will help whenever you need us. Don't hesitate to call," Everett said.

"I know and I appreciate it."

"Maximus is all ready to go. Good luck on the nanny search," Everett said.

he Meeting Place, a business that rented out rooms for gatherings or office space, was where I'd chosen to do the interviews instead of my house. I wasn't a big fan of letting just anyone into my space.

I'd chosen one of the smaller office spaces that contained an oak desk with a tall black leather chair behind it and two cushioned, oak chairs in front of it, in the middle of the room. Adjacent to the desk were windows that gave a fantastic view of the hustle and bustle of downtown Sable Falls.

After getting Maximus settled in his stroller next to me, I placed my notepad and folder of applications in front of me. I'd scheduled four interviews, each one hour apart, giving me time to ask all my questions, get a feel for the applicants, and take a quick breather between them.

I heard a faint knock on the door.

"Come in."

"Mr. Northcott?" the older woman said as she entered the room.

I stood to greet her.

"Miss Anderson?"

She smiled, "Yes."

I extended my hand and we shook.

"Please take a seat."

I waited for her to settle in her seat, then I said, "So tell me about your experience with newborns."

"*T*hank you. I will contact the nanny service." I smiled and shook the hand of the third interview of the day.

She smiled and left.

I rubbed my temples and looked out the window at the people walking and driving by. My brain was tired.

"Maximus, you might be coming into the office with me," I said out loud to a soundly sleeping Maximus.

He'd slept through most of the interviews. Honestly, he hadn't missed anything. I'd already decided to contact the nanny agency and let them know that their services would not be needed. I'd been extremely detailed about the type of person that I needed to care for my son. None of the previous three fit the bill.

The first woman had a family and couldn't work overnights even though I'd specifically said I needed live-in help. The second woman wore a low-cut shirt and a short skirt. Her answers were flirty and I could've sworn she'd winked at me. She was a no-go. I was looking for someone that would be dedicated to my son – not someone to smash. The third person was a guy. I was not opposed to a male caring for Maximus, but he wasn't what I had in mind.

I had no idea it would be so hard to find someone.

Just as I'd checked my watch to see how much time I had before the final interviewee arrived, I heard a knock on the door.

"Come in," I answered while looking down at the paperwork to see the name of the last person.

I stood to greet the person and almost lost my balance when I realized who it was.

"Angel?"

"Xander? Hi!" she said as a huge smile spread across her face.

She looked terrific in a cream pantsuit with a deep purple blouse and leopard print pumps. When I saw her on the plane, she'd worn her hair up in a tight bun. Today she'd let it down and wore it big and curly. She was stunning. The scent of fresh-cut roses and lavender followed her into the room.

"Hi!" I extended my hand.

We shook hands.

Trying to form my words while at the same time making sure I wasn't dreaming, I looked down at the application and saw the name, Angelica Saint Rose.

Angel...

"Puh..." I cleared my throat, "Please take a seat."

I couldn't actually believe she was one of the people I was interviewing. As I listened to the first three candidates, I'd thought back to the way she'd handled Maximus on the plane and I'd hoped I would find someone that I vibed with the way I'd vibed with her.

"So, you're a nanny?"

"I've babysat kids my whole life..."

"I remember you mentioned your cousins on the plane," I interrupted.

"Yes, I babysat my younger cousins as a teenager. When I was in college, I worked as a caregiver for a family with two small children for two years," she answered.

"Why did you leave that position?"

"I started taking the classes towards my major, which were significantly more difficult than the gen ed classes. I needed more time to study, plus they moved away from the area."

I looked at her resume, which was included in the paperwork I'd received from the agency.

"You graduated from Talmadge University with a degree in business management. Why are you looking for a position as a nanny?"

Talmadge was one of the most prestigious universities on the east coast, located here in Sable Falls.

"I'm great with children. I want to do something that brings me joy."

I went through all the same questions I'd asked the other candidates. She blew me away with each answer she gave. She didn't get familiar like we'd met before. She conducted herself like it was a real interview. She was the best candidate I'd interviewed.

I pretended to take notes on my paper, but I knew that I would offer her the position as soon as she'd walked into the room. She was who I had been looking for in all the other candidates.

"You know that I need live-in help and that sometimes my work schedule fluctuates depending on what's going on in the restaurants," I said.

Something in her expression shifted. It was a quick reaction, but I didn't miss it.

"Restaurants?" she repeated.

"Yes, I'm the Vice President of Culinary Development for the Molitor Restaurant Group. I'm a trained chef, but I'm not in the kitchen anymore. Sometimes if there is an event or the introduction of a new menu, I will spend time in the restaurants making sure it all goes well. Does the live-in aspect bother you?"

"Absolutely not. I knew you needed live-in help coming in. Your fluctuating schedule is not a problem at all," she said.

Maximus started to whimper.

"Is that my friend?" she asked.

"Yes, I think he's hungry."

"May I?" she asked, motioning towards Maximus.

"Sure."

Reaching into her bag, she produced a small bottle of hand sanitizer. After vigorously rubbing her hands together, she fanned them.

"Okay," she smiled.

I picked Maximus up from his stroller and passed him to her. I had no idea why I was comfortable with this stranger handling him, but I was. The way Maximus gave a sleepy smile let me know that he didn't mind either. She sat back down in her chair.

"Hello, beautiful boy," Angel cupped Maximus' head in both her hands and spoke to him.

I started preparing him a bottle after handing her a burp cloth.

"It's been what? A week? He's grown!" Angel observed.

"Yes, it's been a little over a week. He had his checkup today with the doctor and he is doing great," I proudly announced.

"I can tell. Are you and your dad are having a good time?" Angel spoke to Maximus.

If Maximus weren't only a couple weeks old, I would've sworn he was flirting. He was doing this weird half-smile thing that he'd never done with me.

I continued to prepare the bottle while watching her with him. She handled him so gently, but not like he was fragile. She was comfortable with him. The way he hadn't cried since she'd held him let me know that he was comfortable with her.

"I want to offer you the job, Angel."

She paused and looked up at me.

Her beautiful eyes were mesmerizing.

"Really?" she smiled.

"Yes, you are comfortable with Maximus. You understand that my schedule will be hectic sometimes, and he seems to be comfortable with you. Do you need time to consider the position?"

"No, I don't. I accept," she smiled. "Will I need to do another interview with Maximus's mother?"

"No, his mother passed shortly after she gave birth to him. That's why I was on a plane flying across the country with a newborn."

"Oh," she put her hand to her mouth. "I'm so sorry. That was so insensitive of me!"

"No, it wasn't. How could you have known? She and I had agreed to co-parent, but we were living very separate lives. So, all of this was thrust upon me. I'm creating and learning as I go. Does that change your mind about the position?"

"No! I'm excited about working with this little guy."

"I will contact the agency and let them know that I've offered you the position. Once I hear back from them, we can schedule a start date."

"Sounds good," Angel smiled.

*A*NGEL
    "I can't believe you accepted a nanny position," my friend Leona said.

"When did you apply to be a nanny?" my other friend Tatum asked.

"Before I came back to Sable," I answered.

"Why?" Tatum asked.

"I needed a way to support myself. I knew I couldn't stay here long with Jacory moving in. I needed a job to pay for a place."

"Don't do that," Tatum scolded. "You know you could've stayed here forever. We would've made it work even with Cory here."

17

Jacory was another one of our friends from college. After college, he'd moved to Washington to work for a start-up tech company that had grown large enough to have offices in other states. He was moving back to Sable Falls and into the house with Leona and Tatum.

"Yeah, babe, we could've cleaned out the room over the garage if we had to. You didn't have to make such a…" Leona paused.

"Weird, rash, crazy-ass decision," Tatum interjected.

I'd always described my friends by using a friendship spectrum. Leona was the sweet, comforting friend on one end of the spectrum while Tatum was the no-nonsense, no-holds-barred friend on the other end of the spectrum. I fell somewhere in the middle. Since the day we were put together in a tour group during college orientation in our freshman year, we'd been friends.

Leona, the real estate agent, was the prim and polished girl who came from a certain level of money and loved a good luxury brand. However, she didn't look down her nose at people who were less fortunate than her. She freely gave and shared. She was a gorgeous, tall and lean woman with long, thick natural hair, pretty copper skin, and a killer smile. Men often thought she was dumb because she was so pretty, but many had been fooled.

Tatum the financial analyst's family was not as financially secure as Leona's. However, she knew how to save a dime and still have fun. Her parents checked her credit score the way they checked her grades at the end of the semester, making sure she stayed on course to purchase a home straight out of undergrad. She appeared to be carefree and spontaneous, but she always had a plan even if it looked effortless when she did it. She was a naturally beautiful woman; medium height and plus size with curves for days. She kept her natural hair braided and tucked under custom wigs. I couldn't remember the last time I'd seen her hair out. She rarely covered her tawny hued skin with makeup, but she enjoyed a good beat with the rest of us. She didn't learn about luxury brands until we all became friends, but now, she was the master of mixing high-end with low-end fashion and making it look fierce.

They were like the sisters I'd always wanted, always having my back and loving me regardless of my flaws. We'd experienced the best and the worst of life together.

"What about the position at the restaurant?" Tatum asked.

"They called and offered me the position after I left the nanny interview. I declined their offer."

"WHAT! That was the position of a lifetime, sweetie. You've talked about it since you finished culinary school," Leona said.

"So, you don't want to be a world-renowned chocolatier?" Tatum asked.

I sat back on the couch, feeling like someone had let all the air out of my giddiness balloon. I'd walked into our place excited about the news I had to share with them – finally, some good news - but their reaction had me wishing I would've just kept the news to myself.

"Right now, I want to be Maximus' nanny," I answered.

"What the fuck is a Maximus nanny?" Tatum threw her hands in the air in frustration.

"The baby's name is Maximus!" I shot back.

"Oh, I don't know shit about domestic work. My ancestors worked way too hard to give me choices. I thought it was like the highest level of nannydom or some shit," Tatum answered.

"Tatum!" Leona scolded while tilting her head and widening her eyes.

"Fine, continue Mary Poppins," Tatum said.

"I'm done," I said and started to leave the room.

"No, no, babe. Please don't leave. Just help us to understand," Leona pleaded.

"Ain't no use in getting frustrated with our questions. Your family is going to ask the same ones. You might as well practice your answers on us, Nanny McPhee," Tatum said.

I hated how brutally honest Tatum was sometimes, but she was right. I sat down on the couch, trying to compose myself before I spoke, "I don't want to be in a kitchen. I don't want to see chocolate, and I definitely don't want that position at Le'Soul – not right now anyway."

I'd finally said out loud what I'd known to be true for months. The thrill and my passion for food was gone.

"I just need to do something that I'm good at that will bring me some level of peace."

Leona and Tatum flanked each side of me on the couch and put their arms around me.

"It's okay, babe. Do what makes you happy. We are just happy you are back here with us," Leona said.

"I agree," Tatum smiled.

They put their arms around me and hugged me.

"Thank you," I choked out before the tears started to fall.

I sat silently wrapped in both of my best friends' arms while I cried for what felt like the millionth time.

Eventually, Leona got up to get me a tissue, but Tatum didn't move.

"You know I love you and I only want what's best for you," Tatum finally spoke.

"I know."

I took the offered tissues from Leona.

"Here, babe, your phone is ringing," Leona said while handing my phone.

"This is BG," I said while standing up. "Might as well get this conversation over with."

"Hey BG," I said cheerfully, trying to mask the sorrow I felt. "I accepted a job offer!"

"What! Congratulations! Is it at the restaurant you talked about?" BG asked.

I stepped into the backyard and closed the door behind me.

"Ummm...no?"

"Oh, you decided to go with another one? I know you had more than one option," she responded.

"No, BG. I took a job as a nanny."

My grandparents had raised me because my mother chose to travel the world as a background singer for various singers and groups. She was never in one place long enough to give me any semblance of a consistent life, so BG – best grandma – and Papa had taken me from her.

"Angelica – what are you talking about? Is nanny a position in the kitchen that I don't know about?" BG questioned.

"No, I was hired to care for an infant named Maximus."

"I'm confused. You told me you were finally taking the interview with the restaurant there you'd talked about for years."

"I did. I took the interview with Le'Soul. It went well. They wanted to hire me, but..."

"Chocolate is your passion, Angel."

"It used to be..."

"It still can be..." BG countered.

"I still haven't been in the kitchen since," I paused to swallow the lump that instantly formed when I attempted to finish my sentence.

"Don't you think it's time? Your Papa wouldn't want you to stop doing what you loved because he isn't here anymore."

"Papa was the reason why I pursued the culinary arts. He was the joy I found in the kitchen. I don't want to do it without him. It doesn't feel right."

I dabbed the tears with the balled-up tissue in my hand.

"Joy comes from within, Angelica. It doesn't come from the outside. You know that," BG stated.

"Well, the joy died when Papa did. I went to the interview at Le'Soul, and it felt like my chest was going to cave in when I walked into the kitchen. Everything there reminded me of Papa."

"You knew him for twenty-seven years. I knew him for twice as long. He was the love of my life, so I understand the loss, believe me. But we all have to move forward. He wouldn't want you to throw your future away," BG argued.

"I'm not throwing my future away," I cried.

My Papa was my world. As early as I could remember, he and I were in the kitchen, creating something delicious and listening to music. He was a self-taught chef but could compete and win against any formally educated chef. Papa had a knack for taking flavors that typically shouldn't be mixed and creating works of art. He was also great at confections, which was where I'd developed my love for chocolate. I made my first truffle under his tutelage. Spending time with Papa in the kitchen was more enjoyable than going outside to play with my friends.

After finishing my degree in Business Management, I went to culinary school intending to become a chocolatier. After culinary school, I was offered the opportunity to study with one of the world's top chocolatiers. His main restaurant was in London, but he traveled to his other locations in Paris, Australia, and Brazil. I took the position and moved to

London to study and work. I frequently called Papa to tell him about the fantastic food, the fresh ingredients, and new culinary adventures.

After my first year in London, I'd planned on going back to the States because Papa was having some health issues. Papa told me if I left because of him, he wouldn't speak to me. I knew he would eventually speak to me again, but making empty threats was not his thing, so I'd stayed. I also figured that he was okay if he told me not to come home. Late in the night, I received a phone call from BG informing me that Papa had passed unexpectedly. I'd returned home from London and hadn't been back in the kitchen since.

"I'm not saying that I'm never going back to the restaurants, but not right now," I announced.

It felt good to finally tell her. She'd asked me about getting into the kitchen so frequently that I felt pressured to take the interview with Le'Soul. Maybe she would give me a break – at least for a little while.

She was quiet for several minutes.

"Okay, you're grown. You have to do what you feel is best. That doesn't stop me from still offering my advice because that's my job. I just want you to understand how it feels to me. I've lost Quincy, and now I have to watch you go down a path that you certainly didn't plan for, and to what end?"

"Maybe my path will lead to some peace? Maybe happiness? Hopefully, healing."

"I hope so," BG replied.

"Anything has to be better than right now. I at least have to give it a try."

"I'm always here if you need me," BG said.

"I know..."

We quietly held the phone. I knew BG had more to say. She surprised me by asking the question that meant the conversation was over.

"Who can love you better than you?"

"No one can love me better than me," I replied with the phrase she'd made me repeat since I could talk.

"Exactly. No one is going to love you or treat you better than you. You are responsible for your own happiness and orgasms," she finished.

BG was a clinical sexologist. She often included sex and pleasure in the list of things to make a person feel better.

"Yes, ma'am. I know."

"I love you, my precious Angel."

"I love you too, BG."

3

Angel

"*D*amn, are you sure this is the address?" Tatum asked, looking at the large, white, modern farmhouse with black trim and a large three glass-paneled front door we'd pulled in front of. The lawn was beautifully manicured, adding to the curb appeal.

I double-checked my text messages and my email.

"Yep, this is it."

"Wow...what does he do?" Leona asked.

"He works for Molitor Restaurant Group," I answered, still admiring the enormous house from the car window.

"Does he know you are a savant in the kitchen?" Tatum asked.

"We didn't discuss anything culinary related."

"Mmm hmm," Tatum mumbled.

"Well, at least you have something in common with him, so that's good," Leona said.

"Maybe he'll convince you that you should be in the kitchen and not wiping some brat's runny nose," Tatum said.

"Tatum!" Leona scolded. "We are being supportive, remember?"

Tatum rolled her eyes.

I dialed Xander's number.

"Hello?"

"Hi, Xand...Mr. Northcott. It's Angel. I'm outside."

"Xander works and okay. I will come out and help you with your things."

"That's okay. I have two of my friends with me to help if you don't mind. They just want to make sure I'm okay."

"I understand," he chuckled. "I will open the garage."

"He's opening the garage," I announced to the car. I took a deep breath. "Okay, let's do this."

We all climbed out of the car as one of the three-car garage doors opened and out walked Xander.

"Cheezuz," Leona said under her breath but loud enough for us to hear her.

"You ain't neva lied," Tatum whispered.

Xander wore a black sleeveless t-shirt with black sweatpants. The t-shirt's ribbed material clung to his chestnut-colored chest like it loved being there. His sweatpants hung low on his waist and he had the baby monitor clipped to his pocket. His dark hair looked to be freshly faded and lined up along with his mustache. Bushy eyebrows framed his face complete with dark eyes, a negro nose, and a strong jaw.

Xander smiled as he approached, showing off his beautiful set of white teeth.

"Xander, these are my friends, Leona and Tatum."

"Nice to meet you," Xander said, extending his hand to both.

"I can take that trunk," he said, pointing to the back of Leona's truck, "and show you to your room."

He lifted the heavy trunk with minimal effort and started back towards the house with all three of us in tow. We walked past one car and one SUV parked in the garage. He continued into the house, past a vast white and gold kitchen. I had to pause to take in the kitchen's grandeur. The large marble island was long enough to have six stools neatly tucked under it. It was the most massive kitchen island I'd ever seen. The top of the line six-burner stovetop, double oven with French doors and a double-sided refrigerator, were white with gold handles and knobs. The backsplash and all the countertops were white marble with faint black veining throughout. The beauty of the kitchen took my breath away.

I caught up to the group just as Xander announced, "This is your room. It shares the bathroom with the room next door, which is Maximus' room."

He put the trunk in the corner of the room.

"Make it your own. I will grab the other bags out the truck," Xander smiled.

"Oh my gawd," Tatum whispered. "I see why you took this position."

"This house is gorgeous, and this room is huge! Did you see the pool and that beautiful pergola?" Leona asked.

"I saw it. It's beautiful back there," I whispered back while still examining the room. All the furniture was white with gold accents, like the kitchen, with a soft pink color on the walls. It had a very minimalistic vibe to it. I liked it. French doors led to a small balcony that gave a breathtaking view of the pool and a view of the city.

The girls followed me into the large bathroom with a standalone tub, walk-in shower, and double vanity, through the other door to a room decorated in light blue, gray, and white.

"Shhh," I paused when I saw Maximus sleeping soundly.

"Ohhh..." both girls whispered.

"He is gorgeous," Tatum gushed. "Look at all that hair!"

"He's a little angel. Look at those chunky cheeks. I will kiss those all day," Leona added.

"He's not a brat at all. I take that back," Tatum said.

We slowly backed out of Maximus' room and back into mine.

"This is a walk-in closet," Tatum said after opening one of the doors along the wall.

"Are all the boxes in the truck coming in?" Xander asked after placing a box on the floor.

"Yes, we are coming to help," I said.

"I got it. Get familiar with the house," Xander said and left the room.

"Okay, Mr. Xander," Tatum whispered.

*A*fter Xander unloaded all my things, the girls left. He gave me a formal tour of the five-bedroom house, which included his room, down the hall from mine and Maximus' rooms, a home office, and two guest bedrooms. It seemed large for one person, but maybe he didn't live alone. I hadn't asked. I just knew he wasn't in a relationship with Maximus' mom.

"I purchased this house out of undergrad with a small inheritance I received from my great grandfather. The house was a foreclosure, and it was in terrible shape, but it was in the area that I wanted to live in. I knew if I put money into it, it would be a great investment. Most of the work you see, my dad and I did it. Some of it was done by the construction company my dad worked for. I've worked on it over the years to get it to where I wanted it," Xander explained.

"It's beautiful. It seems big for just one person. Does anyone live here other than you and Maximus?"

"Thank you. And no, it's just the two, well, three of us now. I got it because my parents live in St. Helane, which is a drive, so when they come up, they stay with me," he answered.

"So, as I told you over the phone, I filled out all your paperwork with the agency. Your direct deposit will be in effect with your first check. These are the keys to the house, the code to the gate, and the keys to the Range Rover..."

"Range Rover?" I interrupted.

"Yes – is that too big? I figured you would be more comfortable in that opposed to the Mercedes coupe since it only has two doors, but if you're more com..."

"No, no...I'm okay," I stuttered.

He handed me the keys.

"Okay, so the car seat base is already installed in the back seat. That took me about two hours on the phone with tech support to get in, but it's secure," he chuckled. "So, if you have appointments or outings, you and Maximus are set. You can also use it for your personal business. It's yours as long as you are employed here." He handed me a credit card. "This is the credit card you will use for gas. There is one on its way with your name on it, but it shouldn't really matter because you're using it at the pump."

He continued to talk, telling me about the cleaning service and the chef, both of whom had their own schedules and should coordinate with me based on Maximus' schedule.

I heard Maximus start to whimper through the baby monitor still attached to Xander's pocket.

"I will get him," I said as I turned towards his room.

"No, you don't officially start until Monday. You don't have to do that," Xander said.

"It's my pleasure. Besides, Maximus and I need to get acquainted and talk about how our days are going to go."

*X*ander
Startled awake by the fact that I'd been sleeping too long and hadn't heard Maximus' cries, I sat straight up in my bed. I looked around, trying to get my bearings, then looked at the clock. It took a few seconds for my eyes to adjust so I could read the numbers.

"Three forty-five?" I said out loud.

I rushed from my room into Maximus' room. He should've awakened by now to be fed. I worried that I had slept too hard and didn't hear him crying. I couldn't hear him crying, which also concerned me.

"What if something happened in his sleep? He's never slept this long."

I heard faint sounds of music coming from his room when I approached the door. I pushed it open and found Angel in the rocking chair, listening to jazz while holding Maximus.

"Hey," she whispered. "I hope we didn't wake you. I know you have to get prepared to start getting up for work."

After rubbing my hand down my face and letting out a huge sigh of relief, I stepped into the room. I'd forgotten Angel was there.

"No," I whispered back. "I woke up and realized he hadn't woken me up to feed him."

"I fed him. He drank about four ounces, I changed him, and we've just been relaxing, watching the moon and listening to jazz," she answered.

I sat down in the chair opposite Angel and Maximus.

"Did he cry loud?"

"He didn't really cry at all. I was awake and heard him whimpering. Don't worry. You didn't sleep through anything," Angel explained.

"I didn't even realize I fell asleep. I remember hanging up from talking to my sister. Then I woke up."

"You have a sister?" she asked.

"I have a twin sister, Tatiana."

"A twin! Younger or older?" Angel asked.

"I'm eight minutes older than her."

"That had to be cool growing up," she smiled.

"It was. She was my built-in best friend. She is living in Austria right now because she plays with the Philharmonic there."

"Really? What instrument?"

"The violin."

"Nice, do you play any instruments?" she asked

"No, I was too hyper to sit still and learn. It was boring to me."

"I've been to Austria. It's beautiful when it's not freezing cold."

"Really?" I said.

"Yeah, I lived abroad after college. Mostly in London, but I did some traveling."

"London, huh? Did you like living there?"

"It was a nice experience," she said.

She adjusted Maximus and rested him on her shoulder and began to rub his back the same soothing way she'd rubbed it when we were on the plane. I couldn't watch her because I felt my eyelids getting heavy.

"Who is this you're listening to?" I asked, trying to shake off the sleepiness.

"McCoy Tyner," she answered.

"Is he a new artist?"

"No, this song, 'Contemplation', is on his album *The Real McCoy*, which was released around nineteen sixty-seven or sixty-eight. He played with Coltrane on some of his more popular songs," she rattled off.

I guess my look of surprise made her clarify.

"My papa, my maternal grandfather, was a huge jazz aficionado. He listened to old jazz acts like Charlie Yardbird Parker and Dizzy Gillespie. He and I spent hours listening to his old vinyl records. Papa said my mother listened to jazz every day of her pregnancy with me, so it was no wonder I liked it so much. They say you are supposed to play classical music if you want your child to be intelligent, but Papa always said play jazz if you want them to understand their soul," she said.

"That's deep. Is jazz your favorite genre of music?"

"I don't know if I have a favorite. I listen to a little bit of everything. Jazz is definitely at the top of the list, but it's more for creativity and relaxation. I listen to other genres depending on my mood. What about you?"

"I'm an old school rap and R&B dude. I can listen to the Isley Brothers, or I can listen to Nas. It depends on my mood like you said."

"Who is your favorite old school R&B singer or group?" she asked.

"That's a loaded question because there were so many to choose from for different reasons. Billy Paul..." I started.

"Billy Paul's voice is as satisfying as spreading room temperature cream cheese on a bagel. It's so relaxing but commanding at the same time."

"Exactly, so underrated, and most people only know him for 'Me and Mrs. Jones', but his voice was amazing."

"Yep, I agree. My papa would put on 'Let's Make a Baby', and I knew it was time to leave him and BG alone," she chuckled.

"So, you grew up with your grandparents?"

"Yes, my mother traveled a lot as a background singer. She still travels as a background singer. She's been chasing her dream of stardom for so long. One would think that her dream would slow down and let her catch it, but it's a slippery one," she chuckled.

"They all live in California?"

"BG and my mother live in LA. We lost Papa eight months ago."

"I'm sorry to hear that."

"Thank you. It's been a difficult time," she said.

"Do you have any siblings?" I asked.

"None that I know of. My mother didn't have any more children, and my father was never in the picture. Is it just you and Tatiana?"

"Just me and Tati. I don't know if my parents could've handled any more. We were quite the handful," I answered.

Maximus started snoring.

"I can put him back in his bed," I offered.

"Sure."

I grabbed Maximus, who was sleeping like he'd worked a full eight-hour shift.

"Thanks for letting me get some sleep, Angel."

"It's my job, right?"

The first week back to work was hectic, to say the least. There were one million emails, condolence and congratulations cards, and gifts. Everyone wanted to pop into my office to say hello and ask to see pictures of Maximus. I checked my phone and text messages a million times the first couple of days, hoping not to miss a notification from Angel concerning Maximus. I had to travel to all four restaurants to check on the staff, and I had to visit the new location to make sure everything was running on schedule.

"Xander, your mother is on the phone," Rocky the receptionist said.

I looked at my cell and realized I hadn't turned the ringer back on after the meeting I'd just finished. I saw the missed call from my mother then quickly scanned my notifications to make sure I hadn't missed anything from Angel. I breathed a sigh of relief when I realized I hadn't.

"Okay," I said and braced myself for the conversation with my parents.

"Hi, Mom!"

"Hey, Xander. How are you? We are having such an amazing time! Your dad and I went ziplining in Bali," she said.

"Ziplining! Where are my parents?" I laughed.

"Living our life like it's golden," my mother sassed.

I smiled, picturing her rolling her neck with her hand on her hip.

"Where are you now?"

"Singapore. We were in Thailand the day before yesterday," Mom answered.

"Enough about us! I saw the pictures you sent of Maximus! He is beautiful! How did Piper do? Tell me everything. I need her number to do the phone camera thing to talk to her and see Maximus. Do you think she will mind?" my mother rattled off.

"Is Dad close?"

"I can hear you, son," my dad's baritone voice blasted.

"Hey, Dad, how are you?"

"Good, son. We are enjoying ourselves," he answered.

"Good. So, the birth went well..." I started.

I told them the entire story about Maximus' birth and Piper's death. There was silence for a few minutes before they said anything.

"Wait, did you say she died?" Mom asked.

"Yes, ma'am."

"There is an emergency number that you could've utilized, Alexander!" Mom yelled into the phone.

"Mom, I..."

"I can't believe you! You've gone through all of that and I didn't know anything? I knew that I would miss his birth, and you and your sister forced me to reconcile with that but to miss his birth and his mother's funeral? What type of mother and father do people think you have?" she yelled.

My mother and father had saved for years to take a year-long cruise around the world after my dad retired from construction. Once I got promoted to VP, I gave them the last chunk of money to make the life-long dream a reality. The trip was already in motion when I found out about Piper's pregnancy. There was no way for them to cancel the cruise without waiting another year before they could possibly do it again. Mom cried about missing the birth of her first grandchild, but I'd promised her I would take plenty of pictures, and then she and I would go back out to visit him once they were finished cruising. I didn't use the emergency number for the cruise line to inform them of Piper's death because there was nothing they could've done. I didn't want to ruin their plans. It was a calculated risk I took. After listening to my mother cry and yell, it appeared that the risk wasn't entirely worth it.

"Mom..."

"Don't Mom me. Here talk to your father. I'm too upset."

"Hey, son," my father said.

"Hi, Dad."

"Congratulations."

"Thank you, sir."

"I understand why you did what you did. Your mother is upset because despite what young adults think, parents don't stop being parents. She would trade her whole life to make sure you and your sister are okay. It wouldn't have hurt us to try this trip again another time," he explained.

"Dad, I know. I made a choice as a man and I stuck to it. That's what you always told me. You and Mom worked hard to give Tati and me the best. I'm not going to keep taking from you without making sure you get something in return. I knew once I got the news that Piper had passed that I probably should've called, but to what end? For you to fight to find a ticket to the west coast to sit at the funeral of someone you didn't know and then what? Sit around here with Maximus and me? It wasn't worth it to me. I'm sorry I hurt her, but we are okay. Maximus has a fantastic nanny, and we will be right here when you are finished."

"Nanny!" I heard my mother scream. "Vincent do the camera thing that Tati taught us."

"I don't know if that works out here, Pearl," Dad responded.

"Do the camera thing or I am going to find someone on this ship with a phone," my mother threatened.

"Dad, how long will you be in port?"

"We will be here overnight," Dad said.

"Okay, I'm leaving work soon. I will FaceTime you so you can meet Maximus."

"Okay," Dad said.

"Alexander..." Mom said in a familiar threatening tone.

"I'm going to call back, Mom, I promise."

FaceTimed my parents as soon as I arrived home from work. They had gotten new phones right before they left for the cruise and neither knew how to use them outside of calling and texting.

"Can you see me?" my dad said as soon as he answered the phone.

"Yes, can you see me?"

"Hey, son!" my dad smiled.

"Hi, Dad. Hi, Mom. I'm sorry!"

They both looked good. Dad seemed to have a little more grey hair around his temples, but I figured that was due to him letting it grow out. Mom was radiant. I'd always believed I had the most beautiful mother in the world. Her caramel skin and beautiful brown eyes kept the secret of her age well. People always asked if she and Tati were sisters instead of mother and daughter. They both looked relaxed and rested even though I could see the worry in their eyes.

"I don't know if I forgive you yet. Show me my grandson and this woman that's the nanny. Does she speak English?"

"Pearl." "Mom." My dad and I spoke at the same time.

"What Black people do you know with a nanny?" my mother sassed while rolling her eyes. "I should be home taking care of my grandchild, but I'm out here with all these people we don't know."

I quickly walked through the house after discarding my jacket and my briefcase. Following the music, I found Maximus and Angel in his room.

Angel smiled. I smiled back and pointed to my phone.

"Mom, this is Maximus," I said and rotated the camera so she could see him.

"Oh my god...he looks just like you when you were his age," Mom said.

"Yep," Dad said, clearing his throat. "He's a handsome fella."

"Look at those fat legs! What is he eating?" Mom asked.

"Everett gave him a prescription for milk from a milk bank. It's a place where nursing mothers donate milk when they produce too much."

"I never knew anything like that existed," Mom responded.

"Yeah, it's tested and it's safe. He likes it and he's growing."

"He has a head full of hair," Dad said.

"You remember the twins were bald," Mom chuckled.

"For years!" Dad added.

"And where is this woman that's taking care of him?" Mom asked.

I saw Angel's eyes get big.

"This is Angel," I said and turned the phone towards her. "Sorry," I mouthed as she smiled and waved. "Angel, these are my parents, Pearl and Vincent Northcott."

"Hi, Mr. and Mrs. Northcott. I'm Angel Saint Rose, Maximus' nanny."

"Oh! Hi!" Mom said.

"Hello, darlin'," Dad said in an octave lower than he usually spoke.

I knew Angel would throw them off a little.

"It's a pleasure to meet you," I heard Mom say.

"The pleasure is mine! I heard you were on a cruise?" Angel said.

"Yes, we are. We are in Singapore right now," Mom answered.

"I've never been to Singapore, but I heard the gardens there are beautiful," Angel said.

"That's what the excursion host told us. We will see them tomorrow," Dad said.

"Oh, and the chicken rice. I had a friend in college from Singapore. She used to make chicken rice, but she said it was better in Singapore," Angel said.

"We will have to try it," Mom responded. "Are you from the Sable Falls area?"

"No ma'am. I'm from Los Angeles, but I went to college here and I've recently moved back," Angel answered.

"What college?" Dad asked.

"Talmadge."

"Dad, that's your alma mater," I responded.

"Absolutely, green and gold for life," Dad said.

"I'm green and gold until I'm old and gone!" Angel cheered.

"That's right!" Dad said.

"Maximus is an absolute joy. He's getting a little cranky because it's time for him to eat. I'm going to go and prepare his bottle. It was nice meeting you," Angel said.

"Nice meeting you as well," Mom said.

"Take care, darlin'," Dad said.

Angel left the room.

"Emmaline ain't gone like that," Mom snickered.

Dad chuckled a little, too.

I shook my head and turned the camera back to Maximus.

"Oh..." I heard my mother say after some announcement in the background.

"We have dinner reservations. The bus to the restaurant is about to leave," my father said.

"Mom..."

"Yes?"

"I'll always need you. You're my girl, and you know that. Everything hit me at once, and the last thing I wanted to do is ruin your dream. I'm sorry. Both Maximus and I are good. After all you and Dad sacrificed for us, the least I could do is be an adult and take care of my business."

"I know your intentions were good. I'm your momma and I want to be the first person you call when things like this happen," Mom said.

"I know. I love you. Have fun, okay?"

"But wait, are you okay? Do you need anything?" Mom asked.

"No ma'am. I'm not going to lie and say that I didn't second guess myself a few times in the past few weeks. This was exciting, heartbreaking, discombobulating, scary, exhilarating, and exhausting all in waves. I have pictures of Piper for Maximus, so he knows her when he gets older. Andrews was her last name, so I gave him that as a middle name to honor her as well. We are going to be okay, though."

"I'm going to start looking at coming home a little early," Mom said.

I knew better than to argue with her.

"Yes, ma'am."

4

Angel

Learning to be the sole caregiver to an infant was a little harder than I thought it would be. The first few days with Xander home allowed us to tag-team Maximus' care. Once he went back to work, reality set in.

I knew the basics of caring for an infant. Still, no one accurately described the sleep deprivation, the loss of memory, and the overall feeling of helplessness when he cried and was inconsolable. There were a couple of times I just couldn't figure out what he wanted.

In the first few weeks, I learned a lot. I learned to sleep when Maximus slept, even if I wasn't tired. I ate when he ate because the opportunity may not present itself for several hours. After a couple days of quick birdbaths in the sink, I learned to take the baby monitor into the bathroom with me and take showers during his first morning nap.

Having a support system of other nannies was pivotal to my survival during those first few weeks. I called one of them freaking out the first week on the job.

"Hey, Betty, how are you?"

"I'm good, Angel. What's going on? I can hear something is wrong in your voice."

"Okay, so, I went to change Maximus this morning, and his umbilical cord is gone. I knew it was hanging off, and I knew not to tug it, so I left it alone. But shouldn't I see it somewhere? I mean, I have looked high and low and can't find that thing anywhere."

Betty laughed.

"Sometimes they fall off and just disappear. I've cared for at least ten infants and have only recovered that thing once or twice. It's elusive. It was probably in his pamper, and you didn't notice it."

"Oh," I exhaled. "So, it's not something that I need to take to his next appointment or something?"

"Girl," she chuckled. "No, it's not."

"Don't laugh, Betty. I was honestly over here freaking out!"

I got the best piece of advice from one of the other ladies that had been a nanny for decades. She told me to try not to lose myself in caring for Maximus. She recommended that I still tried to hold on to one hobby or thing I enjoyed.

I noticed that Xander had a plot of land in the corner of his yard that was sectioned off for a garden. I asked if I could plant a few vegetables in the garden and keep a fresh lavender plant in the window planter outside Maximus' room. He agreed to both. I started keeping fresh flowers in the house and a fresh batch of lavender near Maximus' crib. The herb seemed to help keep him calm.

My first venture out in public with Maximus was memorable. After his one-month checkup, instead of going straight home, I'd decided to walk around the mall just for some exercise and a change of scenery. I packed his diaper bag and put him on one of the cute little outfits that he'd finally grown into because it seemed like all his clothes were huge on him before that.

He was content as I weaved in and out of all my favorite stores window shopping. He drew a lot of attention from the women in the stores, commenting on how cute he was and how much hair he had.

I settled down in one of the seating areas to prepare a bottle and feed him. When I lifted him out of his seat, I felt something warm and wet on my hand. I looked at his bottom and there was green poop all on his backside and down his pant leg.

"Maximus! Oh my god. How were you just sitting in this?"

I put him in his stroller and went to the restroom. It was my first time ever going into a family lounge in the mall.

"Wow." I paused after walking into the brightly lit room. There were murals of children playing, four televisions mounted the wall playing various children's shows, and a couple of rooms labeled, "For Nursing Moms."

"They been holding out," I mumbled.

I rounded the corner and found several family restrooms. The family restroom consisted of an adult toilet, kid-sized toilet, large sink, smaller child-sized sink, and fully stocked changing area complete with a fold-down changing table, baby wipes, disinfectant wipes, and paper covers for the changing table.

After preparing the table, I took Maximus out of his stroller and placed him on top of the table. I carefully pulled his pants off, trying not to get the poop further down his leg, which didn't work. Not only did I get it all the way down his leg, but I got it on his socks.

I unsnapped his onesie and gagged.

"I can't believe this much poop can be inside of something so little."

The onesie was smeared with poop as well. I tried unsuccessfully to get the shirt over his head without getting poop anywhere else.

He didn't complain at all as I cleaned him up with one of his burp cloths. He blew spit bubbles like he enjoyed watching me panic. After getting him cleaned up and his pamper changed, I realized I didn't have a change of clothes for him. He was completely naked except for his pamper.

"Now what am I going to do?" I said out loud, trying to figure out how I would get a naked baby out of the mall and to the car.

I ran through possible scenarios in my head while I used one of the plastic bags to collect his soiled clothes and placed them in the diaper bag.

"I got it!"

I wrapped Maximus up in his blanket and then went to the mall map to find a baby store. Quickly navigating through the people strolling and pausing to look at window displays, I found *Baby Couture*. I rolled my eyes at the name, knowing they were about to charge me an arm and a leg for something that Maximus would likely only wear one time.

Surprisingly the owner of the store was a huge help. The adorable baby clothes were reasonably priced. The owner pointed me to a couple outfits for Maximus and allowed me to use her restroom to get him all changed. I purchased more than I had planned because there were so many cute things in the store.

From that day forward, I learned to pack extra of everything to include socks. I also learned that babies outgrew pamper sizes quickly. The right sized pamper made a world of difference.

⣿⣿⣿⣿ ⠄⠄ ⣿⣿⣿⣿ ⠄⠄ ⣿⣿⣿⣿

*X*ander's work schedule was crazy. He had told me that his hours would be irregular, but he was so busy that he never really saw Maximus. I figured out a way to space Maximus' naps out so he could be awake to welcome his dad home some late nights. Sometimes it worked and sometimes it didn't.

"How is everything going?" BG asked me during our weekly phone conversation.

"It's going well. I feel like a new mother even though I didn't give birth to a child. I've learned so much in such a short time."

"Babies will teach you," she responded. "You were born with a mothering quality, so it's no surprise that you are doing well with the baby. Do you like it?"

"I do," I replied with a smile. "Maximus is an amazing baby. He doesn't give me any problems, really."

I told her about one of my recent mishaps with losing his pacifier. I'd taken the clip off his t-shirt to change him and couldn't for the life of me remember where I put it after I removed it from his shirt. I looked everywhere before I eventually opened a brand new one. After he was down for a nap, I went to the bathroom, looked in the mirror, and realized I'd clipped the pacifier to my shirt and tucked it into my pocket.

She laughed after I told her the story.

"And how is your employer treating you?" BG asked.

"Great. My checks are on time. His schedule has been irregular, but I knew that coming in. He's nice, though. We talk when we can, but for the most part I've been taking care of Maximus and he's been working."

"Do you miss the kitchen?"

I was wondering when she would ask about the kitchen. We'd had four conversations where she hadn't mentioned it. I knew I was on borrowed time when it came to the kitchen conversation.

"I haven't had time to think about the kitchen, BG. I've been so busy just trying to learn how to care for this little one."

"How do you eat if you don't think about the kitchen?"

"Chef Perry is Xander's personal chef. He comes a couple times a week and cooks enough food to basically last us until he returns," I explained.

"Can he cook?"

"He's a great cook. He could probably use a little more salt on some things, but he does well."

"So, you still haven't given any more thought to when you are going to resume your career?" BG asked.

"BG," I said, trying to hide my annoyance. "Right now, this is my career. I don't know if I will ever go back into the kitchen."

"It just doesn't..."

"BG, please!" I argued.

We both held the phone for a few minutes before she spoke again.

"I guess I will talk to you next week," BG said.

I could tell that I'd hurt her feelings when I stopped her from talking about the kitchen, but I couldn't handle it. Well, I probably *could* handle it...I didn't *want to*. I'd finally gotten to a place where I didn't cry every time I thought about Papa. I finally had something else to focus on other than him and all the lessons he'd taught me in the kitchen. Talking about going back into the kitchen wouldn't do anything except snatch the newly formed scab off of my grief wound, that had taken months to grow. I knew I couldn't handle that. If that was all she had to talk about, then I guessed our conversation was over.

"Love you," I said.

"Love you, too," she replied.

. . .

X ander

Before Maximus, I only had to worry about me, so the long workdays didn't bother me. I didn't have to check my phone for missed calls or worry about getting home by a particular time to catch Maximus awake. Working fifteen- and sixteen-hour days left me very little time to spend with him.

Some days seemed to drag on with no end in sight. Then I would receive a text from Angel. No words, just a picture of Maximus doing nothing. Seeing his little face gave me the boost I needed to get through the rest of the day.

The new restaurant's launch was finally wrapping up, so my work would decrease, allowing me more time with my son.

"He's so little," Emmaline said.

"Yeah...he's a baby, so..." I shrugged and adjusted Maximus in my arms.

"Shut up. You know what I mean," Emmaline slapped my arm. "I didn't think I would be this up close and personal to him when he was this small. I thought I would meet him when he came to visit for the first time."

Emmaline had finally made it to the house to visit Maximus. She'd given me several excuses as to why she couldn't make it when Maximus and I had first arrived home. At first, Emmaline was angry after a huge argument she and I had. It started with my need to cancel a trip she'd planned. I never agreed to a trip to Dubai, but somehow, we were going. The argument ended with the whole, "you don't care about anyone but yourself," rant that she usually went on when she was mad. We recovered from that. Then my hectic schedule wouldn't allow us any time to do anything but have quick telephone conversations. Now, we'd both finally had a break, so she was visiting Maximus for the first time. I knew that our schedules were only part of the reason Emmaline hadn't met Maximus yet, though. She was having a hard time adjusting to my single fatherhood.

"So, you said you hired a nanny?" Emmaline asked, looking around.

Just as she finished speaking, Angel walked into the room, carrying a basket of Maximus' folded clothes.

She had her freshly braided hair in a bun on top of her head and she wore a white sweatsuit. Her fresh scent of lavender and honey followed her into the room.

"Oh! I'm sorry! I didn't realize you had a visitor," Angel said after she paused in the doorway.

"It's okay. Come in. Angel, this is my girlfriend, Emmaline. Emmaline – Angel, Maximus' nanny."

"Hi!" Angel placed the basket of clothes on the ground, smiled, and extended her hand.

Emmaline shook Angel's hand but not with as much enthusiasm as it was offered. Angel continued to smile.

"I was about to give Maximus a bath and feed him. I can come back later," Angel said.

"No, go ahead. I don't want to interrupt his schedule. Emmaline and I will get out of your way. Let me know before you put him down so I can say goodnight."

"No problem," Angel replied.

I kissed Maximus and passed him to Angel.

"So...you hired *her* as your nanny?" Emmaline asked after we were in my bedroom.

"Yes. I hired her. Who else would've hired her?" I responded, knowing exactly what she was trying to say.

"She's...what?" She threw her hands in the air looking for the right words. "Nineteen? What does she know about children?"

"She's not nineteen. She's older than nineteen, not that it's any of your business nor should it be a basis of her employment."

"You're okay having a child parading around your house. You don't know her!" Emmaline huffed.

"Em...I don't have the energy for this. She is amazing..."

"Oh, so she's amazing?" Emmaline interrupted.

"With Maximus. Don't do that, Em," I warned.

"Here I am putting my life on hold and changing plans because of your 'break baby' and now you bring another woman into your house! How does that make me look? Did you ever stop to consider how I would feel about another woman living here?"

"His name is Maximus. He's my son, not a break baby. Angel is not

43

just another woman; she's my employee. And let's see," I said while looking up and tapping my chin with my index finger. "When did I have time to consider your feelings? When my son's mother was being admitted back into the hospital after giving birth? Maybe when I had to help plan her funeral for her aunt and her co-workers. Oh, I know when I helped her friend clean out her apartment!"

"That's not what I meant," Emmaline said.

"I needed help with him. Were you going to help me? We've been back almost two months and this is your first time seeing him in person," I said.

"Daycares take care of babies!" Emmaline retorted.

"Not mine, they won't."

"So, you're saying that this is not temporary? Like until you can find a space for him at a daycare?" Emmaline asked.

"I don't work daycare hours, but even if I did, I don't want him in a daycare. So, no, it's not temporary."

"You don't think this is something you should've discussed with me before you did it? Last I checked, I'm your girlfriend," Emmaline argued.

"I should've consulted you about plans to take care of my son?"

"No, I'm not talking about how you take care of your son. I'm talking about bringing some little girl into your home to live with you without letting me know."

"I told you I hired a nanny."

"You didn't say she looked like that!"

"Like what?"

"Don't play with me," she gritted her teeth. "You know what I'm talking about. After you told me you had a baby on the way, I should've just cut my losses."

"I asked you more than one time if my child was going to bring some level of stress to you in this relationship. Every time you told me no. You are arguing with me about making the best decision I could, given the circumstances that were forced on me. I don't have time to properly vet a daycare because of my schedule, nor do I want to. A live-in nanny was the best thing for me. I'm sorry that she's not an old white woman with moles all over her face, but she's the best thing for Maximus right now."

"Fine, Xander," she huffed and folded her arms across her chest.

"It's gotta be, Em."

She'd been so used to throwing grand mal tantrums and waiting for me to give in, but things had changed in the short time Maximus had been in the world. I just didn't have time to take care of two kids; Maximus and Emmaline. One of them would have to grow up, and since Maximus was a baby, it certainly wasn't him.

5

Angel

"**M**an, you are going to have to warn me before you let these big poops rip!" I chuckled while gathering all the supplies I needed to change his diaper. "Whew! What did I feed you?"

Maximus smiled.

"You could've said it would have this effect on your stomach, stinky butt! You are the poopenest kid I've ever met!" I laughed.

He laughed too like he knew what I'd said.

I finished changing Maximus and packed his diaper bag. He and I were going to visit with Tatum and Leona while Xander entertained his guest. He'd called and told me Emmaline would be joining him for dinner. To which I quickly replied, "Man and I had dinner plans with my friends."

I straightened our rooms and strapped Maximus into his carrier, in an attempt to get out the house before Emmaline arrived.

I could tell by the way she responded to me when Xander introduced us that she wasn't feeling me. I didn't know her to dislike her or care how she felt about me, but it was my goal to stay out of her way.

Just as I reached for the door, it quickly opened, and in walked Emmaline. She wore a short, red dress, red pumps, and a long, straight, black wig with a part down the middle.

"Oh, I didn't think you would be here," she said, looking me up and down.

"We were just leaving. Excuse me," I said, trying to get around her and out the door.

"How does one happen upon a nanny position? Did you learn nanny skills at your vocational tech high school?"

I felt myself become irritated instantly. My first instinct was to get on the petty bus with her. Then, in the spirit of keeping my job, I decided to go high like Mrs. Obama taught us.

"There are agencies that provide nanny services," I answered.

"You didn't aspire to be anything other than a baby maid?" she wrinkled her nose and drew her eyebrows in like she was disgusted.

I tilted my head and looked at her.

I mean – how many high roads are there?

"Chef Perry," I called out. "Man and I are gone."

"Good. I don't know why you're here anyway," Emmaline huffed.

"Because Xander hired me? Or because I live here?" I shot back before I could stop myself.

Bitch.

I pushed past her, headed to the garage.

"Angel!" Chef Perry called out once I was in the garage.

"I made you some veggie tacos to go. I remember how much you and your friends enjoyed them the last time," he said.

"Aww, thanks, Chef! I will watch little miss Nevah whenever you and your wife need for more tacos," I smiled.

"Bet!"

Xander's chef usually cooked dinner two to three times a week. One day when Chef Perry and I were talking, he'd told me that his babysitter had fallen through and it was he and his wife's date night. I volunteered to watch their daughter so they could go out. I didn't mind. She was a great kid.

"Have fun and aye – I don't blame you for leaving. I've known Xander for a long time and I still haven't figured out the Emmaline piece," Chef said.

I shrugged.

Xander and Emmaline confused me, too.

"*I*'m going to give you a little bit of this rice and just a drop of the bananas we blended up yesterday. Then you can chase that with some milk. That's a great breakfast, what do you think, Man?"

Maximus and I had been awake for about an hour. I was in the kitchen preparing to feed him breakfast.

"Do you always talk to infants like they can speak back?" I heard come from behind me.

I jumped a little, not realizing Emmaline had obviously spent the night. She had on a sheer black robe that did nothing to cover up the black lace lingerie she had on underneath. Her body was beautiful, but her face and her attitude sucked.

I had replayed our conversation the day before, in my head over and over. I hated it when I got into an argument or confrontation and didn't get the chance to express myself fully. After the fact, I could come up with the best retorts.

She wasn't going to bully me today. I was ready for her.

"If you speak to them as you would any other person, they will learn how to speak properly. He understands me. Isn't that right, Man?" I smiled at Maximus.

"His name is Maximus. Why do you call him man and he's a baby?" she asked.

"His name is Maximus Andrew Northcott, M – A – N, that spells man."

Just in case phonics didn't work for you.

"I guess a child would understand a child," she quipped.

Bitch... was what I said in my head. Out loud, I said, "Having been one yourself many, many, many, many years ago, I guess you would remember that."

"You have such a smart mouth to only be the help," Emmaline said. "The same way you were hired, you can be fired."

"If you were my employer, that might mean something to me, but since you aren't..." I trailed off with a shrug.

"Xander listens to anything I say. He always takes my advice. You really should be looking for another little babysitting gig because when I move in here, you will be the first change I make. The second will be finding a daycare," she said.

I looked at her and turned back around. Xander hadn't mentioned anything about her moving in here. Not that it was my business or my house. If he planned on my employment being temporary, I would hope that he would let me know.

"Good morning," Xander smiled as he entered the kitchen.

"Good morning," I replied.

"Good morning, Man! I didn't get to see you yesterday. I missed you!" Xander gushed as he removed Maximus from his chair.

Maximus responded with spit bubbles and drool. He was always excited when his dad talked to him.

"I was just preparing his breakfast. We will be out of your way in a few minutes," I said while adding the banana to the baby blender.

"I can feed him. I didn't spend any time with him yesterday. I tried to get home before you left, but I got tied up on a call..."

"And then you were tied up all night," Emmaline whispered.

I rolled my eyes and kept doing my job.

"Are you sure? I can feed..."

"I'm positive." Xander smiled, which always did something to me, but I kept my composure.

I finished blending the baby food, made a bottle, and left the kitchen.

*X*ander
I waited for Angel to leave the room before I spoke to Emmaline.

"Is there any reason why you chose to walk around the house barely covered up? You know I have at least one other person living here. Chef or Pieta could come in at any time."

As soon I walked into the kitchen and saw Emma in her lingerie, I nearly lost it. I knew that Angel was just my employee, but I felt a level of respect should be shown to her as someone living in my home. Emma was intimidated by Angel, but I wouldn't allow Emma to disrespect Angel in my house. I didn't want her to feel uncomfortable in a space that I'd given her free rein in. There was not one area in my home that was off-limits to Angel and she knew that. However, she still kept to her area and rarely came into mine.

"I thought it was early, and I could come in here and make some coffee before anyone else was awake. I didn't know your little nanny would be in here," Emmaline responded.

"Is there a reason why you felt the need to engage her? You could've made your coffee on this side of the kitchen and left her alone," I returned while putting Maximus' bib on him.

"I was just trying to get to know her and understand how she handles Maximus. I mean, at some point, we will be able to get rid of her and put Maximus into a traditional daycare. I called the nanny service you used to find her..."

"You did what?"

"I just wanted to know more about the person that was living here with you," she answered.

"That was not your place! How did you even know which agency I used?"

"I saw the folder on your desk. They didn't tell me anything anyway, but I told them that you would be adding me to the contract as a point of contact, then I will be able to handle that on your behalf."

I paused from feeding Man and looked at her. All the memories of why we didn't make it the first time came flooding back. I took deep breaths to stay calm and continued to feed Maximus.

"I also spoke to my friend that's on the board of the ELITE school. He said he could pull some strings and get Maximus in. Once he's in their system, he could stay with them through high school," Emmaline explained.

"You must've fallen and bumped your head. I didn't give you any indication that I would be adding you to anything, Emmaline. That's the same problem we had before. You insert yourself into places or situations where you are were not asked and are not welcome. Angel's employment is none of your business. As I have already told you, *we* don't have any plans for Maximus to go into a traditional daycare. I love the way Angel takes care of him."

"I bet you do..."

"And I don't plan on putting Maximus anywhere where he is the minority. The ELITE school is only three percent black. That's a non-starter – not even a consideration."

"Once we move in together, I just figured we would be making these decisions together. I don't want another woman living in my house, nanny or not," Emmaline said.

I took a spoonful of the baby food and fed it to Maximus. He spit a little out with excitement. We'd just started trying to feed him small amounts with a spoon.

"There you go, Man!" I smiled.

He was growing so fast.

"So, no response to that?" Emmaline said after watching me feed Maximus for several minutes.

"Em," I took a deep breath before I continued, "Right now, the only woman that's living with me is Angel."

She huffed and quickly stood up from the island stool.

"So, you're choosing her over me?" Emmaline growled.

"I'm choosing the safety and well-being of my son over..." I stopped because I didn't want to say something that I wouldn't be able to take back.

"No, finish your sentence. Over what?" Emmaline yelled.

"You need to calm the fuc..." I looked at Maximus. "Aye, you need to be more aware of your surroundings and calm down in front of my son," I pushed out.

She had pushed me to the point of cussing in front of my son.

"You are so spoiled and need everything to be about you when right now, everything is about Maximus. If you feel like you need to compete with my son for my time and attention, you might as well stop because you are going to lose – hell, you lost. We talked about moving in together before I knew that I would have Maximus full-time and definitely before Piper passed. We talked about it – I never agreed to it. Now, my priorities have changed."

"So, what are you saying?" she asked.

I watched, expressionless, as she contorted her face and blinked in an attempt to manufacture some tears. In the past, her tears would have moved me, but I was tired of her theatrics. I was tired of her tantrums. I was tired of her being self-centered. I was tired of her trying to force me to do things that I didn't want to. I was just tired.

I didn't respond. Instead, I gave Man his last spoonful of food and said, "Look at you! You ate all this food! I'm going to need a second job to feed you!"

He spit and cooed like he was trying to respond.

"I'm outta here," Emmaline huffed and stormed out the kitchen.

A few minutes later, she stormed back through the house, fully dressed.

She paused, waiting for me to say something.

"You ready to get dressed?" I asked Maximus and carried him out of the kitchen.

*A*ngel

I tried not to let Emmaline's words bother me, but they did. I pondered them for a couple days after our conversation. I figured Xander would talk to me if he planned on letting me go. However, I didn't really know their relationship dynamics and I didn't know how their pillow talk went. Actually, I didn't understand them at all.

Xander was an amazing, caring, attentive guy who tried to move heaven and earth to make sure the people around him were cared for. On the other hand, Emmaline seemed to be a narcissistic, self-absorbed, unaware, petty-ass bitch.

Maybe it was a case of opposites attract.

"Hey," Xander said after joining Maximus and me outside.

I was tending to my garden, which was doing remarkably well. Maximus was sitting on a blanket in the grass, enjoying the sun.

"Hi," I smiled.

"Man! Did you have a good day today?" Xander asked.

Maximus spat and flailed his chunky little arms.

"He had a great day. We've been out here exploring nature, learning about grass and trees. He likes it out here."

"I can see," Xander answered. "The garden looks great! Chef told me he's used some of the herbs and garlic," Xander said.

"Yep, he has," I said proudly.

Xander's work schedule had leveled out. The new location was basically done and waiting for some last-minute permits, so he was back on a regular-ish schedule. I expected him home by seven or eight every night, and usually, he made that happen.

"How was your day?" Xander asked.

"Busy keeping up with this little guy. He's growing so fast."

"I know he is," Xander responded.

"I have a question to ask you."

"Shoot," Xander said.

"The other morning, Emmaline said that she would be moving in soon, and you were going to put Maximus in a daycare..." I trailed off.

Xander's face had contorted into an angry grimace. I didn't know if he was mad at me for bringing it up or what, but I didn't want to continue until I was sure.

"She said that to you?"

"Yes," I quickly responded.

"When?"

"The day you came in the kitchen and she was here," I replied.

"Emmaline is not his parent, nor is she your employer," he started.

"I know, but she said..."

He growled, "That means that she doesn't make decisions on his care or your employment."

"Xander, I didn't mean to upset you."

"I'm not upset with you – at all. I'm irritated that she would say something like that to you. I wish you would've said something sooner. You've been concerned about your employment for days, unnecessarily."

"I didn't know how to approach it. I don't know how your relationship with her works," I responded.

"Listen to me carefully, Angel, I don't have any plans for you to go anywhere. I need you. I wish there were a less creepy way to say that, but there isn't, so it is what it is. You have been a real godsend to Maximus and me. Even if Emmaline were to move in, which for the record she's not, you wouldn't be going anywhere. If there are any changes in your employment, I will let you know. You won't ever hear anything second-hand. Got it?"

"Got it." I smiled.

"Good. Would you have dinner with Maximus and me?" Xander smiled.

"I would be honored."

"Cool. I have a quick phone call to make, then I will meet you in the kitchen. I think Chef said he made jambalaya?" Xander said.

"Yes, I taste-tested it earlier. It's delicious."

6

Xander

"He may be a little cranky after his shots today, but his weight and everything looks great. He's growing fast. Any concerns?" Everett asked.

"No?" I looked at Angel.

She'd accompanied me to Maximus' doctor's appointment. Since she spent most of the time with him, she knew how to answer all the questions.

"He's the best baby ever born. He's happy, and he eats well. He's sleeping on a schedule not necessarily through the night, but it's a schedule." She shrugged. "I have noticed a slight uptick in his drool, though."

He was always a big slob bucket, so I hadn't noticed there was more of it.

Everett rewashed his hands then pulled Maximus' bottom lip down. He used the tip of his finger to run it along Maximus' gumline.

"He's teething," Everett announced.

"Teething!" both Angel and I said at the same time.

"Yes," Everett chuckled.

"I thought babies didn't get their first tooth until about six months?"

"That's what I read," Angel agreed.

"It varies from person to person. Wash your hands and feel. You can feel them cutting through," Everett instructed.

I followed Everett's instructions, and I felt little ridges on his gums.

"Are you kidding?" I smiled.

Angel handed Maximus to me, washed her hands, and felt his gums.

"Man! Why didn't you tell us?" Angel smiled as her eyes watered. "I'm sorry, his little milestones always mess me up."

"Don't apologize," Everett said. "Caretakers and parents always have similar reactions to milestones."

I smiled, watching her become emotional. She cared for my son like she was family and not a paid employee. He had the best of everything when it came to his care because Angel made sure of it. She knew the differences in his cries. She knew how to make him laugh. She knew when he was hungry, and sometimes, she could just feel when he was awake. One time, she was in the kitchen with Chef and me and said, "I think someone is awake." I went into his room, and sure enough, he was just in his crib quietly, watching the mobile light on the ceiling.

"Xan, can I speak to you for a minute before you go and buy this guy a steak?" Everett chuckled.

"I will take him out to the waiting room and schedule his next appointment," Angel said.

"Thanks, Angel."

She packed up Maximus and exited the room.

"She smells like lavender and coconuts," Everett said after hearing Angel speak to his receptionist.

"I know. She always smells good, and after she handles Man, he smells just like her."

"Is it perfume?" Everett asked.

"I haven't seen any perfume bottles in her room. I think it's just her, but I'm not sure."

"So..." Everett started.

"What?"

"Eviline called Kerry to tell her that you are most likely sleeping with your nanny. She said you told her that if you had to choose, you would choose Angel."

"You know good and damn well I am not sleeping with Angel," I said.

"I know, and Kerry defended you to Eviline. Kerry almost walked it back when she went on your Instagram feed and saw Angel in the background of one of Maximus' pictures. She went on and on about how gorgeous she was and how cute of a couple you two would make," Everett said.

"No one can dispute the fact that Angel is drop-dead gorgeous. Without makeup, hair oil, or lotion, she is easily the most beautiful woman who has ever stepped foot in my house or into my life. However, I'm not sleeping with her. I did tell Emmaline that if she tried to make me choose, I would choose Maximus. Maximus comes with Angel – period."

"You told her that?" Everett smiled.

"I did. I had to call her the other day because apparently, when she was at my house, she told Angel that she was moving into my house. She also told Angel we were putting Maximus in daycare and wouldn't need Angel anymore," I recapped.

"You've got to be kidding," Everett said.

"No, I was so pissed when Angel told me that I couldn't think straight. I called Emma, and she didn't deny anything Angel told me she said. That was it for me. This time it's over for good."

"*What!*" Everett exclaimed with a smile. "She didn't tell Kerry that part."

"I figured that would make you happy. Yeah, man, things have changed so much for me. I knew that Emma probably wasn't the woman I wanted to spend my life with, but she was comfortable to a certain extent. I didn't need to learn her or figure her out. After Piper died, I realized that life was too short to deal with anyone or anything that didn't bring me peace and happiness."

"Is that Angel?"

"I enjoy the peace Angel brings to my life. Pieta, my maid, loves her, and Chef tries to cook dishes to impress her so he can trade her favorite dishes for babysitting credits. She's terrific with Maximus. I can't deny that I'm attracted to her and look forward to going home every day and seeing her. She is my employee, but yeah, she's who I want to be with."

I'd decided to be honest with myself. I knew I didn't hire Angel just because I knew she would be good with Maximus. I hired her because I wanted her near me. It wasn't something I would deny any longer.

"Well, I say get to know Beauty, and I'm glad you got rid of the Beast! You know I couldn't stand Eviline, and she couldn't stand me. Kerry only dealt with her because you did. Now that it's over, we are free! I feel like the black munchkins on *The Wiz*!" Everett laughed.

"I feel good about the decision. I'm ready to move on."

"I'm happy for you. You should bring Angel over to the house so Kerry can meet her. She will tell you what's up for sure," Everett said.

"I just might do that."

*A*ngel
　　"You did so well with Doctor Everett. You are the best baby ever," I said while kissing Maximus' neck.

We were waiting for Xander in the lobby.

"Angel?"

I looked up and saw Calvin, my ex-boyfriend standing in front of the stroller. He looked at me, looked at Man, then looked back at me.

"Wow..." he said and looked at Maximus again.

"Hey, Calvin. How are you?"

"Good, you've been busy," he said. "I guess that's why you didn't return any of my calls. I heard about your grandfather. I wanted to give you my condolences."

I secured Maximus in his stroller.

"Thank you. I have been busy, and no, that's not why I didn't return your calls. We didn't have anything to talk about," I shrugged.

"I see, now. How old is he?" Calvin asked looking at Maximus.

"You two ready?" Xander asked after emerging from the back of the pediatrician's office.

"Calvin, I can sign for that package now," the receptionist said.

Calvin looked at the package in his hand like he'd forgotten why he was in the office.

"Yes, we're ready. Take care, Calvin," I said and navigated around him.

Xander held the door while I pushed the stroller. We walked down the sidewalk to the car together.

"I added his next appointment to your calendar. It's next month," I told Xander.

"Okay, I will block that whole day. We can make it a Man day," Xander responded.

"That will be nice."

After we were settled in the car and pulled from the parking lot, Xander said, "So...Calvin?"

I took a deep breath.

"He and I dated. Actually, he's the last person I dated."

"What happened if you don't mind me asking," Xander said.

"He called it Valen*times* day, so it was doomed to fail," I chuckled.

"Oh, that's all bad!" Xander said.

"It was..."

"You don't have to talk about it if you don't want to."

"No, I had an opportunity out of school to live abroad. He's the type of person who wants to stay close to his family, which means that generation after generation has lived here in Sable Falls. I didn't have a problem with that, but he thought that I needed to pass on my opportunity to live abroad for us to be together. I couldn't do it – I wouldn't do it. The same day Papa died, he called to tell me that he didn't want to be with me anymore," I explained.

"He didn't know about your grandfather, did he?"

"No, I actually got the call about Papa after I spoke to Calvin."

"That was bad timing," Xander said.

"It was horrible timing. I mean, I felt us drifting away, but I didn't think he would quit me over the phone. I guess it was better than quitting me over text," I replied with a shrug.

"Either way is a chump move, in my opinion."

"I can't argue with that," I shrugged.

"You drifted apart because you felt like he was holding you back? Or was it the distance?" Xander asked.

"It was a little bit of both plus he came to visit me when I was in London. I think he thought that since he'd traveled all that way, it entitled him to my body. It didn't. I didn't ask him to come, and I most certainly didn't lead him on to believe that I was going to sleep with him. I didn't want to have sex with him, so I didn't."

"Did he try to hurt you something?" Xander asked, quickly glancing at me then back at the road.

"No, no, nothing like that. He thought he was going to take my virginity," I confessed. "It wasn't his to take. It's mine to give, and I didn't want to give it to him."

"So, you're still..." Xander started.

"A virgin? Yes," I answered.

I waited for Xander to balk or choke or something. Men usually had some extreme reaction when I shared my history. He didn't have a reaction.

He simply asked, "Are you waiting for marriage?"

"Not necessarily. BG is a sexologist, so I've learned about sex and understood my sexuality my entire life. My virginity is valuable to me. I want to save it for someone I want to give it to and not someone who thinks they deserve it because they've put in the time. Calvin thought that since we were together for so many months that he'd earned his way in. When I said no, he told me something was wrong with me because who holds on to it for that long? So, when he saw us..."

"Oh!" Xander chuckled. "Ol' boy thought Maximus was yours – ours!"

"I'm sure that's why he kept looking at Man and said something about me being busy," I chuckled.

Xander laughed hard.

"That's hilarious! Talk about timing! Poor dude. He's all messed up in the head now." Xander continued to laugh.

"Probably," I laughed.

"Talking about a gut punch! That's going to really mess with his ego," Xander said.

"Welp, his loss."

"That's true, and I commend you for sticking to your principles. Do what feels right to you," Xander said.

We rode in silence for a while until Xander spoke again.

"Hey, you want to get something to eat before we go home. My treat?" Xander asked, smiling.

I smiled back at him. "I never pass up free food."

"I need to stop at my office to grab a file I left on my desk, and then we can go get Cajun. How does that sound?"

"Delicious."

Xander

I asked Angel to come up to my office so she and Maximus wouldn't have to sit in the car. I was almost certain the folder I needed was right on my desk, but I didn't want them waiting in the off chance that it was not.

"Your office is beautiful," Angel said, looking around.

"Thank you," I responded while noticing the folder I needed was not on top of my desk. I started doing a mental inventory, trying to recall where I may have placed it.

"Hey, Chef," one of sous chefs from the restaurant below my office said.

"What's up, Chef Daryl?"

"Hey, I saw you come up here. I'm making the banana brûlée again, and I wondered if you would have time to stop by the kitchen and try it again?"

"Give me a minute to find this folder, and I will meet you down there. By the way, Angel, this is Chef Daryl, he's one of the sous chefs downstairs at *Chakula*. Chef Daryl, this is Angel and Maximus."

"Nice to meet you," Daryl extended his hand to Angel.

They shook.

"I've seen pictures of you, little guy. Your dad is proud of you," Chef Daryl said to Maximus.

"I'll meet you downstairs. I just need to locate a folder," I said.

"Cool," Daryl said and left.

"Here it is!" I said after shuffling more folders around my desk.

"If you can, just give me a few more minutes. I need to meet Chef D in the kitchen. He has been working on this dish for weeks and can't seem to figure out. I've been his taste tester. It's the dish he wants to submit to the executive chef for the upcoming promotion selection."

"I'm good." Angel smiled, but it wasn't a genuine smile. I wasn't sure if she was just hungry or tired. We had been out for several hours.

"Are you sure?"

"Of course," she answered.

*A*ngel

I tried to hide the panic I felt when Xander asked me to go to the kitchen. I hadn't been in a kitchen since the interview with Le' Soul. The feeling of labored breathing, chest tightness, and sweaty palms was not something I was ready to experience again.

I should've just said I would meet him in the car, I thought to myself.

The elevator doors opened to the back of the kitchen. The smells of dishes being prepared, the noise of pots clanging and people yelling over each other hit me like a long-lost friend hugging me. It felt nothing like it did when I interviewed with Le' Soul. I smiled and fought back the tears that were stinging the backs of my eyes. It felt like home.

Wow, I just may be okay, I thought to myself.

We walked past all the chefs in their black and white smocks, preparing various dishes for the evening. I saw a couple of apprentices being taught a new technique by the senior chefs as we made our way to the dessert area.

"Okay," Chef Daryl started. "I think I've got it this time."

He pushed the perfectly plated dessert complete with the charred sugar on top, a mint leaf, and a perfect semi-circle of melted chocolate across the counter. Chef Daryl passed both Xander and me a fork.

"May I?" I asked, motioning towards the dish.

"Sure," Chef Daryl answered.

I leaned over the plate, closed my eyes, and tried to take in all the aromas of the dish. It smelled good, but there was one scent that was missing.

"It smells good," I said after stepping back.

All three of us took a sample.

"Dang, it's still missing something," Chef Daryl complained.

"It's closer than it's ever been, but I agree it's missing something. I can't put my finger on it," Xander said.

"A little espresso powder in the mix, vanilla sugar on top – and a splash of fresh lemon after its plated," I answered.

Both men looked at me.

Then Chef Daryl looked at Xander.

Xander shrugged like, "What have you got to lose?"

Chef Daryl stepped away and came back with a bowl of the remaining custard, a lemon, a container of what I figured was vanilla sugar, and a box of espresso powder.

"How much?" Chef Daryl asked.

"To taste," I replied.

"Do you have time for me to put this back in the oven for about ten minutes?" Chef Daryl asked.

Xander looked at me. I smiled.

"Go for it," Xander said.

Chef Daryl sprinkled the espresso powder into the custard. He tasted it looked up at us and smiled.

"Try it now," Daryl smiled.

We both took a small sample.

"Good," Xander said.

"It's great," I agreed.

Chef Daryl quickly put the custard into a small baking dish and placed it in the oven. I tended to Maximus while Daryl and Xander talked.

After the custard finished baking, Chef Daryl cut up some fresh bananas, placed them on top, and then sprinkled the vanilla sugar. He used the torch to flambé the top and crisp up the sugar.

"Okay," Chef Daryl said and passed us two more spoons.

"Wow," Xander said after he tasted it.

"Now it's perfect," I added.

"It is perfect," Chef Daryl said after he tasted it.

"Your suggestion was spot on," Xander said.

"I used to make a version of this with my Papa."

"I knew I knew you from somewhere. You graduated from *The Culinarian Institute*," Daryl said.

I smiled.

"You attended *TCI*?" Xander asked.

"I was a year behind you. Hell, this is your recipe," Chef Daryl said.

"No, it's not my recipe, it's yours, and it's delicious. Thank you for allowing me to try it."

"Thank you, Chef," Chef Daryl responded and placed his hand over his heart.

It had been so long since someone called me Chef, it really felt good. I returned the gesture.

Xander

Angel and I loaded Man into the car and headed in the direction of our dinner location. I kept running the kitchen scenario through my head. I had no idea why I hadn't asked Angel what type of job she held before she became a nanny. Or did I ask her? I know her resume didn't list anything about *TCI*. *The Culinarian Institute* was one of the most prestigious culinary schools in the world. It was nearly impossible to get into and even harder to graduate from. Graduates of *TCI* had open doors and a curated career that graduates from other culinary schools were not afforded. Their network of restaurants and graduates was extensive, and they took care of their own.

"So, you weren't going to tell me you are a chef?" I asked after I couldn't take it anymore.

"I was a chef. I'm a nanny," she responded, which grated my nerves.

"What does that mean? You graduated from *TCI*. That carries a ton of weight in the industry, Angel. It's an enormous accomplishment."

"I guess I would've mentioned it at some point. You never asked," she shrugged.

"You guess you would've...I never..." I couldn't get my words together; I was so irritated. "You've been in my house for four months, almost five. We had all sorts of conversations. You never once mentioned that you are a chef. That bothers me."

"I've been employed by you for almost five months, we've had all sorts of conversations, and you never asked," she retorted as she shrugged.

I looked from her to the road and back to her again. I was mad at her and at myself for not asking more questions. How was she able to omit that whole part of her life? Was I so self-involved that I had no idea who was living in my house? I'd called Emmaline self-absorbed, but obviously, I was too. I never thought to ask her about her life before me. She'd told me bits and pieces about her grandparents but thinking back, she asked more questions about me than I ever did about her. I was living with a *TCI* graduate. That was like an actor living with an Academy Award winner. I didn't know if I was more upset with Angel or myself.

"I wasn't trying to keep anything from you, Xander," she said quietly. "It's not a secret. It's just hard to talk about."

"Did you have a problem in the kitchen once you graduated or something?"

"No, actually, I moved to London and worked with Patrico Oliver."

"The chocolatier?"

"Yes, I was Chef Pat's apprentice. Papa encouraged me to take the position even though he was getting older and started having health issues. Chef Pat and I were working well together, and I was learning and traveling a lot. I passed on an opportunity to go home to check on Papa because Chef Pat and I were invited to a huge event. Chef Pat allowed me to debut my own bonbon at the Elite Chef event. Papa encouraged me to go because that was a huge deal for a second- or third-year chef to debut a confection at the event. A couple days after the event, Papa died."

She paused and took a deep breath before she continued, "I should've gone home instead of going to the event. When Papa died, it felt like the joy of cooking and creating died with him. I couldn't go back to London. I went home to California and stayed until my mother and grandmother encouraged me to come back to Sable Falls. I applied to the nanny agency because I knew I needed a job. I figured caring for children would keep me occupied enough not to think about the kitchen. I interviewed with a restaurant, but I knew at the interview that I wasn't ready. At the interview, they showed me the kitchen and I had literal chest pains. It felt like I was having some sort of attack. I kept my distress to myself, but I was lightheaded when that interview was over. I tried to go back to the kitchen because everyone in my life told me I should."

"When I walked into that interview room and realized it was you and

Man, it just felt right. It felt like maybe I was getting a chance to try something new, give myself space to heal, and help someone in the process," she finished.

I felt like a jerk for forcing her to talk about it.

"I'm sorry, Angel. I know your grandfather's passing has left a huge hole in your heart."

"I miss him so much. I just didn't know grief felt like this."

"Grief is impossible. I want to say it gets better, and it does, but it's not like it will be better tomorrow," Xander said.

"It has been hard, but it's no excuse for me keeping secrets. I wasn't trying to keep it a secret. It's just every time I wanted to talk to you about it, a lump so large formed in my throat and stopped me. Plus, honestly, I didn't want you to be like everyone else in my life and tell me I needed to be back in the kitchen. I'm sorry. I should've told you," she said.

"I'm sorry for getting upset. Your chef status doesn't have anything to do with your ability to care for Man. I just felt like we were cultivating a friendship..."

"We are. That's why I should've said something," she interjected.

"I want that too, but I have to be more giving. I never asked you about your passions or what you wanted to be when you grew up. That's not how friendships work. So, let's say from this point forward, we will get to know each other, friend," I said.

"I would like that, friend," she agreed.

"I have so many questions about your time at *TCI* and with Chef Patrico, but we have time, right?"

"We do." She smiled, which made my stomach drop for whatever reason.

"How did you feel in the kitchen today?"

"Actually, I didn't have any of the panicky feelings I had before. It felt just like home. I almost wanted to grab my smock and start making some truffles," she said.

"Truffles? Is that your specialty?"

"I love to make truffles because you don't have to worry so much about them being pretty or perfect, they just have to taste good. Bonbons are my specialty. They have to be pretty and taste good."

"What dessert did you debut at the Elite event with Chef Patrico?"

"My raspberry, chipotle, and extra dark chocolate bonbon. Chef Pat put them on the menu at his restaurants," she said.

"That's an interesting flavor profile. It sounds delicious."

"I will have to make them for you one day," she said.

"Promise?"

"Promise," she replied, smiling.

⠿⠿⠿ ⠶ ⠿⠿⠿ ⠶ ⠿⠿⠿

"*H*ave you ever eaten here before?" I asked Angel.

"No, I always said I wanted to come down here, but I never have. I've heard great things about it, though," Angel said.

"It's one of my most favorite places to eat. There are a couple things I think you should try. Can I order for you?"

"Of course, Chef. Go for it," Angel said.

Since I wasn't in the kitchen anymore, people didn't call me Chef very often, but I enjoyed hearing it.

Deciding against a traditional restaurant, I took Angel to Food Truck Row. It was a local event held at Sanders Park on the west side of town, once a week in the summer months. Every Thursday, food trucks lined several blocks within the large city park to sell their food. Only the best of the best food trucks were invited for the event. Food Truck Row was a Sable Falls favorite.

Between my work schedule and my ex-girlfriend feeling like eating from a food truck was beneath her, it had been some time since I'd visited Food Truck Row. The layout had changed some, but there were still lights strung from all the trucks to illuminate the area as the sun was setting. They'd placed long benches and tables in the center of the trucks for seating.

A band was setting up on the stage in the distance, while people placed their lawn chairs in front of the stage, preparing for the performance.

Angel chose one of the benches and parked Man's stroller next to her. I went in search of the Cajun truck.

"What can I get for you?" the young lady asked once it was my turn to order at the *Geechee Boys* food truck.

"I'll take two shrimp po' boys, two small gumbos, one shrimp etouffee, and one crawfish etouffee. Oh, and extra crusty bread, please."

"Got it."

I paid for the food and went and sat with Angel. She was feeding Maximus some baby food concoction she'd developed for him. According to her, he wouldn't eat vegetables, but if she mixed the veggies, meat, and fruit together, he would gulp it down. Man had no idea he was eating food prepared by a trained chef.

"I decided to go ahead and feed him because he's not going to be happy watching us eat," she said.

"Yeah, and with those two teeth, he'll be chewing food in no time."

"I know, right? I can't believe his teeth are coming in already!" Angel said.

"Alexander Northcott, as I live and breathe!"

"Hey, Leslie!" I said as I stood to greet my old college friend.

We hugged.

"Matt, this is one of my dearest friends from college, Xander. Xander, this is my boo, Matt," Leslie said.

Matt and I shook hands.

I couldn't keep up with who Leslie was dating. By the next time we saw each other, she would probably have a different man on her arm.

"This is the baby?" Leslie asked.

"This is Maximus," I answered proudly.

"He is so handsome. I heard about everything from Kerry. I hope you got my gift?" Leslie said.

"I did. Thank you. Oh, I'm sorry. This is..." I started.

"Oh, I know who this is," Leslie said.

I thought she was about to spew some of the garbage Emmaline was spreading.

"Chef Angel Saint Rose. You broke my heart when you turned down the head confection chef position we offered you," Leslie said.

I looked from Leslie to Angel.

"I had already accepted another offer." Angel motioned towards Maximus.

"I see. I thought I lost you to another restaurant, but I didn't. I lost you to these handsome fellas, huh?" Leslie smiled.

"You did," Angel answered.

"Xander, I don't know if you know this, but Chef Saint Rose is a brilliant chocolatier. I personally know of three other restaurants that had been courting her. That raspberry and chipotle bonbon that you made at that event with Patrico was epic. We've tried it more than once in my kitchen and still can't figure out," Leslie said.

Angel smiled.

"I'm learning about her culinary acumen. She helped one of my sous chefs with his dish tonight after he and I had tried that dish at least a half dozen times," I replied.

"I'm not surprised. I tried to get her before Patrico snatched her up. Then I heard that she was coming back stateside. I moved heaven and earth trying to get her at Le'Soul." Leslie smiled and winked at Angel.

Angel smiled back.

"Le'Soul is any chef's dream position. I just wasn't ready to go back into the kitchen. It's been a tough few months."

"No need to explain. I will let you have your evening, but Chef, since I know you are around, can I call on you sometime? I would love your opinion on confections my chef is working on ahead of us opening my next location," Leslie said.

"It would be my pleasure," Angel smiled.

"Number forty-four," I heard in the distance.

"That's our number," I said.

"Here, let me walk with you," Leslie said and tucked her arm in mine. "Matt, can you be a darling and order our food from the vegetarian truck?"

Matt nodded obediently and walked in the other direction.

"You've already tamed him, I see," I said as we walked to the food truck to retrieve my order.

Leslie waved dismissively. "Meh – he'll do for now."

"So, what's up?"

Leslie leaned in and said, "I heard you were sleeping with your nanny; she's gorgeous and smart. Congrats."

I pulled away and looked at her.

"I know it's not true, but I wouldn't blame you if you did," she pulled me back in. "The congrats are for moving on. Run, babe. Don't look back.

That thing you had with Emmaline was a catastrophe. I like Emma, just not for you. She never understood who you were for real. I'm so glad it's over. Also, Chef Saint Rose has the talent to become a legend. She calls herself a chocolatier, but she is a beast in the kitchen, period. I wasn't just trying to get her to be my chef. I wanted her as the face of my brand. She's that talented," Leslie said.

"Really?"

"Hell yeah. I don't know how you ended up with her, but with your skill and her talent, you both could run the Sable Falls restaurant scene to include Le'Soul. I'm just glad we're friends," Leslie said.

"So, the restaurant you interviewed with was Le'Soul?" I asked Angel after I arranged our food on the table.

"Yes," Angel answered, "You and Leslie are friends?"

"Yeah, we went to college together. We started in the same restaurant together."

"She is an amazing and inspiring woman. I dreamed of working at the only Black female-owned restaurant in Central Market. The timing just wasn't right," Angel said.

"I understand."

"Oh my gawd," Angel held her hand to her mouth. "This po'boy is amazing!"

"I told you it was good," I said and bit into my sandwich.

We ate all the food I ordered then I went back to the truck to order two sandwiches for us to take home.

On the ride back to the house, Angel said, "So why did you leave the kitchen?"

"I was chasing money. The VP position was supposed to provide me with more money and less work. That didn't pan out. I do make more money, but I'm working just as long and hard. I never described food as my passion. I always said it was something I was good at. Now I find myself sort of floating, almost lost sometimes when it comes to the culinary world. I don't necessarily miss the stress of the kitchen, but I do miss the joy of the kitchen. I didn't really start missing the kitchen until I had a moment to pause and think. I realized food was my passion."

"Yep, sounds like passion to me," Angel confirmed.

"What about you? Do you want to go back into the kitchen?"

"I have no idea. That's a change because, before today, I would've said no. Now, I'm not really sure. Today was a good day," Angel said.

"In the spirit of the discovery stages of our friendship, what other restaurants were courting you?"

"Brenan's, Michaux, and Holiday," she rattled off.

"Those are all the top restaurants in Central Market. I started at Michaux."

"Yeah, if I had to choose, I would've chosen Le'Soul. Leslie pushes cuisine into places people never thought it could go," Angel said.

"She gave you a compliment similar to that," I revealed.

Angel smiled.

"So, in the spirit of our friendship discovery stage," Angel started and paused. "Nevamind."

"No, go ahead and ask. I'm an open book," I encouraged.

"Okay," she said then took a deep breath. "How did you have a baby momma and a girlfriend? Are you a cheater, Friend?"

I choked on my spit.

"If that's too far," Angel rushed out.

"No," I laughed after I cleared my airway. "Emmaline and I had broken up. Well, Emma and I are broken up."

"Say what now? You introduced her as your girlfriend," Angel said.

"I did, but we aren't together now. It wasn't working," I explained.

"Could it be because of the sleeping bundle of joy in the backseat? I mean, a baby by another woman would cause quite a strain on a relationship," Angel remarked.

Again, I laughed, "No, and for the record, I didn't cheat on Emma. She and I were not together when I met Piper."

"Was it a let's give each other space and then get back together situation or were you really broken up?" Angel asked.

"Really broken up. I had no plans on us getting back together. Emmaline started dating another guy almost immediately. I was single when I got with Piper. I met Piper at a conference, and we hooked up. It was just supposed to be fun. Then she was pregnant," I explained.

"Wow, so this really had been a different year for you, huh?" Angel said.

"That's the understatement of the century!" I chuckled.

"Okay, just so I'm clear. You got back with Emmaline after you found out about Man?"

"Yes."

"Why?" Angel asked.

"I realized I was missing something in my life. I thought it was her, so I got back together with her. I quickly realized she wasn't what was missing. Her being back in my life did not fill the void I was feeling. In all honesty, it intensified the yearning for something else," I explained.

"What is that something else? Let me guess – the kitchen," Angel said.

"Yep, discovering, creating, cultivating and introducing new culinary creations. Satisfying people's palates with delicious food. So, I'm moving forward."

"Forward is a good direction. I didn't like her. I guess I can tell you that since we are friends," Angel confessed.

"None of my friends liked her, so you're in good company," I admitted.

7

Angel

"I think I left his pacifier on my desk in my office," Xander said while trying to calm Man down. He was sleepy but was fighting it like a champ.

I found the pacifier under paperwork that caught my attention. I quickly read over it. I grabbed the paperwork and the pacifier and went back into the living room.

"Here's his pacifier," I announced while giving the pacifier to Man. "I've given him the title of the baby weight champion of sleep fighting."

"That's hilarious and true," Xander chuckled.

"Hey, I wasn't being nosey, but I saw this on your desk. What is it?"

I passed the paperwork I found on the desk to Xander.

"Oh," he shrugged and gave the papers back to me. "It was an idea I had a long time ago. I wanted to open my own restaurant down in Central Market."

"Ethos?"

"The spirit of a culture or community," Xander said.

"That's dope."

"Thank you. I was looking for something in my office and came across that old paperwork. I hadn't looked at those plans in years."

"It looks like you had a huge portion of it already thought out."

"I did. There was a space in Central Market that was available for quite a while. It would've been the perfect spot. It had a second floor that overlooked the marina on the bay, patio seating, and an area for live music. I'd made up my mind that I would move on it then I took the VP position. I said I would stay in management for a couple years to get some experience. That was five years ago."

"The design mockup is so unique. I've never seen anything like it. I love the sections," I said pointing toward the mockup, "like this one is for a more upscale experience. While this one looks like a more family-sharing type experience."

"I wanted it to be a full experience, a farm to table concept with the freshest local ingredients and hire and train homegrown chefs," Xander said.

"You don't want your own restaurant now?"

"I was at work the other night thinking about how many of Man's milestones I am missing. Ethos came back to mind. I was thinking how much energy I put into making someone else's dream great, in the meantime, leaving nothing for Maximus. I could expend the same energy into my own stuff and leave something for him when I'm gone. But..." He waved it off like the idea was absurd.

"But what? Xander, this is absolutely something you can accomplish."

"I had picked the idea back up a couple years ago. Emma didn't think it would do well because there are so many restaurants here, so I stuck with the sure thing."

"Visionaries should only share their plans with those who can help them see the big picture. Never share your plans with those who have no sight. They can only discourage or hinder you."

"That's profound," he said.

"It's true. Only share your dreams with people you know can help you fulfill them. I learned that from Papa. So what there are other restaurants here. There isn't a restaurant here that you are running, Chef. There's no restaurant here that could hold a candle to Ethos. It would be the premier restaurant in Sable Falls, even if it wasn't in Central Market. I think you should reconsider it," I finished.

"I could turn the tables on you, Chef. I know that life dealt you a hard blow when your papa died, but I also know that there is a fire inside of you that is burning to be released. I know you dream about new recipes and new ways to manipulate chocolate. What's holding you back?"

"Wow, so just like that, it's on me?"

"Just like that," he responded.

"How do you know what I dream about?"

"Greatness doesn't go away, it's in you," he said.

I smiled.

It was true. The recipes never stopped coming.

"You know, I've been thinking about this more and more since we were in the kitchen at the restaurant. I know what's holding me back."

"What is that?"

"Fear..." I answered.

"Of failing?"

"Of succeeding and Papa never knowing that I actually made it. He was the only one that understood what life as a chef was like. He understood when I said the chocolate wasn't tempered enough or the Hare à la Royale turned out fantastic when we served it with foie gras in a vol-au-vent."

"You made Hare à la Royale? Did it really take three days?"

"Yes, but it was worth every hour. The hare was so tender, and the vol-au-vent was flaky."

"That sounds delectable. French cuisine was never my strong suit, but I love it."

"What's your favorite cuisine?"

"Southern American is my favorite and my specialty."

"Oh, yeah? What's your dish?"

"I'll tell you if you do me a favor."

"A favor? Does it involve firearms, black masks, or flashlights?"

"What!" he laughed. "No, it's not a reconnaissance or recovery mission."

"Okay, then shoot."

"But wait, if it did involve those things, would you consider it?"

"Yeah, I was just wondering if I would need to take these braids out so the mask would fit over my head."

We laughed.

He held my hand and said, "Cook dinner with me."

Those were the sexiest words a man had ever said to me. Cooking for me was love, and if a man wanted to cook with me, it was like making love. I couldn't even conceal my reaction to the zip of electricity that shot through me when he said it.

"I would love to cook dinner with you, Xander," I barely breathed out.

Xander

Angel and I agreed on a menu of roasted duck breast and crispy leg confit with a peach sauce, roasted seasonal vegetables, and bonbons for dessert. Angel wanted to take me to a place that she guaranteed would have the freshest ingredients for the meal we were preparing. The location was on the southside of Sable Falls, and we lived on the northside. We settled into a pleasant conversation during the forty-five-minute drive.

"Why did you become a chef? Why does food preparation appeal to you?" Angel asked.

"My mother was a caterer when Tati and I were growing up. She said she thought staying home with Tati and me was what she wanted, but by the time we were three, Mom put us in daycare and started working," I laughed.

"She wasn't trying to be at home all day with two kids, huh?"

"No, we were a handful. As we got older, Mom had to force Tati to help her in the kitchen, but I'd always enjoyed it. She wasn't classically trained, but she could take a can of butter beans and a flat from a chicken wing and create magic. She can make anything taste good. I overheard my mother and her friends talking about a man who could cook would always be able to pull a woman. I was at that age where I was into girls and needed to know how to impress them, so I enrolled in a home economics class in high school. I was the only guy in the class, and I immediately understood what my mother was talking about."

"The girls were feeling you, huh?" Angel poked me in the arm with her finger.

"I mean," I shrugged. "One of our dishes in home ec was sloppy joe. The teacher gave us a recipe to follow, but I learned how to make it from helping mom in the kitchen. I added a few more spices to my mix and some ketchup and sugar to pare down the tomato sauce's taste. It was a hit. All the girls liked it. At first, I thought I liked cooking because of the attention I received, but I quickly learned that I loved food because of its joy. Good food makes people happy because cooking is a manifestation of the human soul. We put emotions and our vision of the world on each plate."

"Yes! The reactions are everything," she said.

"So, is sloppy joe your dish? You told me you would tell me later," she smiled.

"No, I can prepare a mean sloppy joe, don't get me wrong, but my favorite dish to prepare is jerk pork ribs. I make them with a ginger-based barbeque sauce."

"Ginger based? Any sweetness?"

"Guava."

"Oh yum," she said.

"Why did you choose chocolate?"

"It's delicious, easy to manipulate, and it makes people happy. The look of sheer joy on a person's face when they open even a small box of truffles or bonbons is priceless," she smiled.

"What kind are you making for dessert?" I asked.

"I haven't decided yet. I'm going to see if they have any of their signature rum on the farm. If they do, I will use that for one of them."

"They have rum there?"

"Yeah, in small batches sometimes. Wait until you see this place. It is unbelievable," she said.

After ten minutes of driving down a winding country road, a large gate appeared in front of us. *Eberly's Farm* was etched above the open gated entrance.

"This is it," Angel smiled.

I followed the road to a large ranch style house with a screened-in porch.

We got out of the car. I retrieved Man from his car seat. Angel secured Man in the carrier that strapped him to her chest. I grabbed his diaper bag backpack.

A tractor driven by a large black man appeared from behind the house. He parked the tractor and got out.

"There's Garrett," Angel excitedly announced.

"As I live and breathe," Garrett said after only taking what seemed to be two large steps to cover several feet of space between him Angel.

Garrett was at least six-foot-six, roughly three hundred and twenty pounds, John Coffey looking dude. With his denim overalls and wheat Timberlands, he could've easily passed for a lighter, younger, version of *The Green Mile* character.

His voice had a deep rattle like a set of Bose speakers with the bass on max.

"Garrett, it's so good to see you," Angel replied as they embraced.

His giant frame completely swallowed Angel and Man.

"You look fantastic," Garrett bellowed as he examined Angel from head to toe.

"Shut up," Angel smiled.

I watched their interaction closely to determine if he was someone I needed to be concerned with.

"And who is this?" Garrett asked, looking at Man.

"This is Maximus. I'm his nanny and this is Xander, Maximus' dad. Xander, this is Garrett and this is his farm."

It felt like my whole forearm fit into Garrett's gigantic hand when he extended it to shake mine. We exchanged pleasantries.

"Garrett, Xander is also a chef. We are looking for some ingredients to make dinner."

"Okay, tell me what you need," Garrett responded.

"We need a good duck, some vegetables, and I need a bottle of rum if you have any."

"Oh, I have all of that. Follow me," Garrett rumbled.

We followed behind Garrett. I couldn't help but admire all the rows of neatly planted crops, all the large green and yellow farm equipment, and the land as far as the eye could see.

"How much land do you have and how long have you been farming?" I asked.

"Since I was born. I'm a fourth-generation farmer. My great-great-grandfather started with forty acres, and my great grandfather added on another hundred and twenty. My father added sixty, and now I have a total of three hundred acres. Not all of it is cleared yet, but we are working on it."

"That's amazing."

I was impressed.

"Thank you," Garrett responded.

"When I was in school, I always came out here to get the best ingredients for my projects. Garrett is the best-kept secret in all of Sable Falls," Angel said.

I had never heard of Garrett or his farm.

We followed him past cattle grazing in a large field, a corral of sheep, and a large chicken coop.

"Man has never seen animals out and about like this," Angel said.

"Me either!"

I felt like a kid. I had so many questions but didn't want to sound silly asking them. I was mesmerized.

"You'll have to come back when little man is older so he can ride the horses," Garrett said.

"Horses?"

"Yeah, you want to see them?"

"Yes, I love horses," I smiled broadly.

We walked into the large white stable with several stalls on each side. Each stable contained a horse. Several workers were milling around delivering hay to stalls or brushing the horses' manes.

"They are in right now because the vet is coming to visit but they are usually out in the pasture like the rest of the animals," Garrett explained.

We stopped at one of the stalls in the middle of the barn.

"This one is Eve," Garrett said while rubbing the mane of a chocolate-brown horse. "She will be the first horse in our family to enter into the Sable Falls derby."

I motioned to touch her.

"She loves attention. Go ahead and touch her," Garrett instructed.

"She's a thoroughbred?" I asked as I rubbed her soft mane.

"Yes, she's my pride and joy," Garrett smiled.

"I've never been to the derby," Angel said.

"Well, I will have some seats in the owner's area. If you want to come, let me know," Garrett offered.

"That would be nice," Angel smiled.

We followed Garrett out of the barn.

"I'll go and get your duck, then you can look around and choose from the vegetables we have," Garrett said.

"All of Garrett's animals are free-range and organically fed. This would be perfect for that farm to table concept you had in your business plan," Angel said.

I smiled, "Is that why you wanted to come here?"

"I wanted fresh ingredients for dinner, but yes, I wanted you to meet Garrett. He doesn't work with any of the restaurants in Central Market, so you would be the only one with access to his farm. Plus, Ethos, a black-owned company, would be doing business with Eberly Farm, another black-owned company. That's the very definition of ujamaa – cooperative economics. You know one of the Kwanzaa principles," Angel smiled. "I also wanted you to taste his rum. You could have it in limited or seasonal supply just like the menu."

Since our discussion about Ethos, she hadn't said too much more about it. However, she'd dropped hints like leaving The Culinary magazine opened to an article about a black chef who opened a restaurant in his hometown. His seats were filled every night, and he received rave reviews for his food. She'd also sketched a logo for Ethos that was so perfect. It was as if she'd read my mind. When I asked her about it, she blew it off and said, "Oh, I was just doodling."

"Here you go," Garrett said after handing both Angel and me each a highball glass.

"Oh, I already know I want the five-year, but go ahead and taste them, Xander," Angel encouraged.

Garrett poured me a shot from the first bottle.

"This is the seven-year rum," he said.

I smelled it before I tasted it.

"I can smell the oak." I swirled it around in the glass. "It's not cloudy." I sipped it.

"This is some of the best tasting rum I've ever had."

"Thank you," Garrett responded.

I had the same response to the other two bottles.

"I will take a bottle of each."

"I got you. Now let me show what I have in the field. I just got some golden beets that are so sweet," Garrett said.

"Oh, those would be nice grilled," Angel said.

"I also have some black Russian tomatoes," Garrett responded.

"I've never tried a black Russian tomato," I said.

"They are black on the outside and green on the inside," Garrett explained.

Garrett led us to the field and plucked one of the tomatoes from the vine. He pulled a pocketknife from his pocket and cut the fruit open. He gave both Angel and me a half.

I bit into the tomato expecting the same taste as a regular tomato. I was pleasantly surprised.

"This is great. It has a slight spicy and smoky flavor."

"Yes, it's like sweet and tart then spicy and smoky," Angel described.

"It's part of the beefsteak family, so it has a meaty flavor," Garrett responded.

We tasted several other vegetables before Angel settled on the ones she wanted for our dinner.

"Thanks for everything, Garrett," Angel said.

We had a plethora of fresh vegetables and everything else we needed for our dinner, including four bottles of rum.

"It was good seeing you again, Angel. It was nice meeting you, Xander," Garrett said.

"Same here," I said and extended my hand.

We shook, then Angel, Man, and I headed back to the city.

"So?" Angel asked as I navigated us down the winding country road.

"I'm impressed," I admitted.

"I knew you would be."

"Thank you. It felt like a field trip. I had a good time and learned a lot," I said.

"Of course," Angel smiled.

*T*he day after we visited Garrett's farm, Angel and I moved around in the kitchen seamlessly, like a choreographed dance. It was almost as if we'd been in the kitchen together before, but it was our first time. Man sat in his swing, happily chewing on his teething toy.

Angel prepared her dark chocolate, rum, and Coke bonbons before she started on the grilled mixed vegetables. Watching her laser-focus while preparing the chocolate was like watching a painter paint a masterpiece. She was meticulous with each splatter of colored white chocolate that went into the mold before she topped it with the dark chocolate. She knew precisely how much liquid to put into the mold before applying the last layer of chocolate. I could barely prepare the duck because I was so fascinated watching her work.

"Here, taste this," Angel said, holding a spoon partially dipped in chocolate up to my mouth.

She watched me intently, moving her eyes from my lips to my eyes and back to my lips, waiting for my response.

"Mmm, that's delicious," I said.

I wanted to take the spoon and lick it clean.

"That's quality chocolate. I have a guy here in town that produces the chocolate for me. He's one of the best around," Angel said.

"Try this," I said after dipping a tasting spoon into the peach sauce.

She closed her full, luscious lips around the spoon, causing my dick to twitch. I took a deep breath to calm myself down.

"Oh my gawd," she moaned, snapping me out the trance I'd fallen into watching her lips. "That is exquisite! I can taste the slight spice from the habanero, but it balances the sweetness perfectly."

I watched her tongue quickly lick away any remnants of the sauce on her lips, wishing I could take care of that for her.

"Thank you," I smiled.

I hadn't been complimented on my food in a long time.

I finished preparing the duck and then set the table with my best plates and lit the candles in the middle of the table on each side of the fresh flowers.

After taking a shower, I changed into a pair of black slacks, black loafers, and a black button-down shirt.

I plated the food while Angel and Man were in their rooms changing.

Angel appeared with Man on her hip. She had on a long pink sundress that looked good on her brown skin. The low cut of the dress showed just enough cleavage for me to fantasize about later. I involuntarily licked my lips, wishing I could taste her. I couldn't take my eyes off her. Utterly spellbound, I watched her put Man in his highchair. I couldn't take my eyes off her. She was breathtaking. I shook myself back to reality in enough time to pull her chair from under the table.

After retrieving our plates from the kitchen, I sat them down and said, "Bon appétit."

"Bon appétit," she repeated.

We both tried everything on the plate before we spoke.

"This duck is perfect," Angel complimented.

"Thank you, Chef. These vegetables are grilled to perfection. The addition of the black caviar is smart and delicious."

"Thank you, Chef," she replied, smiling.

We maintained a food-related discussion during dinner.

"Okay, I'm ready for this dessert!" I said after clearing the plates from the table.

Angel returned to the table with a small plate with two bonbons on it garnished with some cocoa powder and a mint leaf.

"Okay, it's almost been a year since I prepared these. Before you taste it keep in mind, I'm an artist, and I'm sensitive about my – you know the rest," she chuckled. "I'm just kidding. Give me your honest opinion. Don't bite it. Just put the whole thing in your mouth."

My mind went straight to the bedroom when she said that, but I kept my composure. I picked up the perfectly formed chocolate confection.

I popped the first one in my mouth and bit down. Immediately the flavors of chocolate, Coke, and rum all mixed together in my mouth to form a perfect flavor harmony. None of the ingredients overpowered the other. It was one ethereal bite.

"Angel, that is the single best piece of chocolate I've ever tasted in my life. I'm not just saying that because you made it. I'm telling the honest to God truth."

She smiled. I saw some tears form in her eyes, but she didn't let them fall.

"Thank you, Xander."

I popped the other one in my mouth. I wasn't sure what it was because she made it while I was out. I immediately tasted caramelized bacon and maple syrup.

"I taste bacon and syrup. It's sweet, savory with just enough salt. It's exquisite."

"Thank you. It's been so long since I've shared this with anyone. It's like a part of me is starting to feel again after being numb for a long time. I'm so glad we did this."

"I know the culinary world was you and your Papa's thing and I'm not trying to take that space that you have carved out for him, but I would love to share this with you. I would love to be the one you can talk to about truffles, bonbons, and anything else you want to talk about."

"I would like that very much," she said barely above a whisper.

I reached for her and we embraced. I rubbed her back when I felt the wetness from her tears on my shirt.

I'd thought about having her in my arms. Feeling her close to me, holding on to me, felt one hundred percent better than I'd ever thought. I didn't want to let her go.

"Let's set a date twice a month. We will cook together and come up with new exciting culinary things to try. How does that sound?" I asked.

"That has to be the most enticing invitation I've ever received. It sounds irresistible," Angel said.

8

Angel

"**D**on't say I ain't never gave y'all nothing!" I said and placed the box of truffles and bonbons on the counter.

I'd arrived at Leona and Tatum's place. Xander was working late, making sure a huge catering event at one of the restaurants went off without a hitch, so Man and I spent the evening with my friends.

"Don't tell me this is what I think it is," Tatum said.

She rounded the kitchen island with Man on her hip after taking him out of his car seat. Despite her initial thoughts about me being a nanny, she'd fallen in love with Maximus. Anytime I took him around, she was always the first and last to hold him.

"What do you think it is?"

"Are these truffles – and bonbons!" Leona excitedly asked after opening the box.

"Oh my gawd!" Tatum said after popping one of the salted almond truffles in her mouth. "This is delicious! Angel! You made chocolates?"

"I did," I said as I smiled at her.

Leona ate one of the espresso-shot dark chocolate bonbons.

"Oh, I've missed these so much!" Leona said.

"What made you make them?" Tatum asked.

She grabbed two of each flavor then sat down on the couch with Man.

"Wait, let me grab some wine," Leona said.

She brought over a bottle of wine and three glasses.

"Sorry, Maximus, you can't have any of the good stuff," Leona said.

Maximus spit some bubbles like he was attempting to respond. His two bottom teeth had finally cut through, making him even cuter than he was before.

"Xander and I cooked together."

Both girls sucked in air.

"You went into the kitchen?" Leona asked.

"So, he knows you're a chef?" Tatum asked.

"Yes and yes. We were out together after taking Maximus to his doctor's appointment. He had to stop in the kitchen because one of the chefs wanted him to taste something. Long story short, that chef remembered me from *TCI*, and then the same day, we ran into Leslie from Le'Soul."

"Wow," Leona said.

"I know, right? So, I had to explain to him why I stepped away from the kitchen. He was a little irritated with me at first because I didn't tell him, and I completely understood that. But we talked it out and he understood. He asked me to cook with him, and now I feel like I'm getting my mojo back."

"Cook with him...as in food? Or sex?" Tatum asked.

We all laughed.

"Not sex, although." I fanned myself. "Being that close to him in the kitchen was definitely a turn on. I can't deny I like him."

"Pay up, Booch!" Tatum yelled.

"What?" I looked at both my friends.

"When I first saw him and the way he didn't look at you at all, I knew he was feeling you. It was like he was working hard at not being attracted to you. I told Lee and she didn't believe me. I bet her that new Gucci belt she just purchased, that you were going to fall for him just like he already had for you," Tatum explained.

"I don't know why I took that bet," Leona huffed and got up from the couch.

She returned with a black leather belt with the Gucci symbol in colorful stones.

"I can't stand you," Leona said to Tatum and gave her the belt.

"Whatever! This is going to look great with my outfit when we go out with Jacory next week."

"You think Xander's attracted to me?"

"I know he is," Tatum said. "Men are so obvious. I was concerned that he just wanted to smash. Now I know he doesn't want that, he wants you."

"I do like him, but how silly is that for the nanny to fall for the boss?" I whined.

"Girl, first of all..."

"Ut oh, there's a list," Leona laughed.

"Damn straight, there's a list. First, you ain't no damn nanny. You are a badass culinary genius," Tatum said.

"Okay?" Leona added.

"Second, you're single, and he's single since he got rid of that chick that was teetering on the edge of an ass-whooping."

"Oh, cause as poised as I am, we don't go for folks messing with our people," Leona said.

"Okay? Why not see which way that thang lean?" Tatum said.

"To the left, right, or straight up," Leona said.

I laughed and shook my head.

"Third and certainly not least, why not be happy? Why not? You deserve it!" Tatum finished.

"Happiness and more! By more, I mean sex," Leona laughed.

"Kick grief and sadness to the curb. Let that beautiful hair down and live and little," Tatum added

"Y'all are both crazy," I laughed.

"But, are we lying?" Tatum said.

X ander

I smiled, looking at Maximus's picture in a pageboy cap, a bowtie, and suspenders with a colossal number five on his chest. Angel had just texted it to me. She'd been taking pictures of him every month for his monthly milestone. She found something cute to dress him in and pinned a number to his clothes to indicate how many months he'd just turned.

He usually gave her a hard time not wanting to sit still for the shots, but she always managed to capture a great image. He was not necessarily sitting still and smiling at the camera, but it was still a great picture.

"Xander!" Ian Noble said as he approached my table.

I stood to greet him. and we embraced.

"It's good to see you!"

"What's up?" Kingston Wright said, coming in behind Ian.

Kingston and I embraced.

We all sat down at the table.

I'd met Ian and Kingston during my early culinary years. Ian was working at a restaurant in Vegas when we met. Kingston and I met at a culinary exhibit at a conference in Atlanta. There weren't many black chefs in the industry and many of us stayed connected through the Black Culinary Society.

The BCS was one of the only culinary groups founded by and existed to serve black people within the culinary industry. We held quarterly meetings to discuss the changes in the culinary world. We planned for our yearly scholarship event to raise money to send talented black youth to culinary school. The BCS also offered apprenticeship opportunities to up and coming chefs. I was allowed to work with one of the greatest culinary minds through The BCS apprenticeship program. After the quarterly meeting that was held in Sable Falls, Ian, Kingston, and I had decided to go to Le'Soul for dinner.

"Well, if this isn't a table of deliciousness," Leslie said, looking around the table.

We all stood to greet her.

"And all gentlemen. Please sit. I have the kitchen preparing you a tasting menu. It's going to make all of you regret that you didn't take me up on my offer...*any* of my offers." She winked and walked away.

"She hasn't changed," Ian laughed.

"Not at all," I laughed.

"Ms. Leslie asked me to bring this over."

The waitress placed a bottle of top-shelf bourbon on the table and gave each of us a glass.

"She said, enjoy. It's on the house," the waitress said and walked away.

I poured everyone a glass.

"What's new with you?" I asked Kingston.

"*Wright Now*, the food truck and restaurant, are doing well. Running them both is kicking my ass," Kingston responded.

"Running a restaurant ain't for no punks," Ian said.

"I say that all time. Definitely not for the faint of heart. I did take a short break to attend a friend's wedding in Punta Cana. It was a nice break," Kingston said.

"A tropical vacation sounds good," I added.

"It was," Kingston paused and smiled, "An excellent trip."

Both Ian and I knew what that smile meant.

"How are your restaurants? I know the show is doing well," I said to Ian.

"Life is good. I can't complain," Ian responded.

"How is the family?"

"Everyone is good. Speaking of, welcome to the dad club," Ian said.

"Thank you. He's been the best thing I've ever done in my life."

"I hear you," Ian said.

"How is single fatherhood treating you?" Kingston asked.

"Honestly, I was only with him by myself for about three weeks. That was hard, you know, after his mother passed, but then the second best thing I've ever done is hire his nanny. She is spectacular with him."

"A nanny?" Kingston asked. "That's got to be like living with your mother, right?"

"Oh, you've obviously not seen his nanny," Ian chuckled.

"You commented on the Instagram post and said congratulations," I reminded Kingston.

"Wait, you talking about the recent picture you posted with the female holding him? That's your nanny?" Kingston said. "I thought she was your lady."

"No," I stated sadly.

"No, as in she's in a relationship, so she's off-limits or no, but you're working on it?" Ian asked.

"I'm working on it," I admitted.

"Cheers to that," Ian said and picked up his glass of bourbon.

Our food came and filled the entire table with a sampling of everything Leslie had on the menu. Her executive chef was a fantastic cook.

After we finished dinner and our table had been cleared, I said, "I wanted to run something past the both of you. I've been thinking about Ethos again. I think I am ready to start making some moves towards opening it here in Sable Falls. I just thought about the amount of time I've spent making someone else's dream a reality and how much time I spend away from Maximus for nothing. If I have to be away, I want it to be because I'm building a legacy for him."

"I hear you. And like I told you when you first mentioned the idea years ago, I think it's innovative and smart. I would love to shoot one of my shows from the restaurant once you open it," Ian said.

"That would be dope. I remember you mentioned something about having guest chefs. Put me down to do that. I would love to support as long as you come to my spot and do the same," Kingston said.

"I can do that guest spot whenever you need me there. An episode of At Home with Ian would be great at Ethos."

"If we don't uplift and support our own, who will?" Ian said.

"Exactly," Kingston agreed.

heard the sound of high heels clicking against the floor before I looked up and saw Angel walking towards me wearing a white, long-sleeved dress that stopped mid-thigh. She had on white heels that strapped around her ankle. Her braids were up in a top bun, and she wore more makeup than I'd ever seen her wear, but she was breathtaking. I kept staring at her trying to formulate the words to tell her how beautiful she looked.

"Are you sure you are okay with Maximus if I stay overnight with Tatum and Leona?" she asked.

"You are stunning, Miss Saint Rose," I replied.

"Thank you!" She blushed. "You didn't answer my question."

"Of course! It's your weekend off. Go and have some fun. Maximus and I will be just fine. Won't we, Man?"

He was too busy bouncing in his bouncer.

"He agrees," I chuckled.

"Okay, well, I'm off. I will see you later?" Angel said.

"Man and I will walk you out."

I took Maximus out of his bouncer and picked up Angel's overnight bag. She carried Maximus while I followed her to the garage.

After placing her bag in the backseat, I reached for Maximus.

"Are you sure?" she asked, hesitating to give Maximus to me.

"I'm positive. Here, take my credit card and buy a couple of rounds or dinner or something on me."

"No, Xander!" she argued.

"Yes, Angel. Please, it's the least I can do. You've sacrificed so much of your time for us. Go and let your hair down."

She took the card. "Thank you, Xander. Take care of my favorite person until I get back."

"I will."

"Man, take care of my other favorite person until I get back, okay?"

She kissed Maximus and passed him to me.

I pulled her in for a hug.

"Have fun, okay?"

"Okay," she replied as she smiled.

She got into the truck. Maximus and I watched her back out of the garage.

"Well, it's you and me, buddy. Let's see what we can get into."

*H*ello?"

"Um...hello, Mr. Northcott?" I heard a male's voice, but it was Angel's phone calling me.

"Yes? What's wrong? How did you get Angel's phone?"

"This is Jacory, I'm Tatum and Leona's roommate. I was out with the girls, and they've been drinking. I was going to take them all back to our place, but Angel keeps talking about she wants to come home."

"I can come and get her. Is she okay?"

"Stop, Leona. Sit down," he said away from the phone. "She's fine. Just a little inebriated. She doesn't really drink, so it didn't take much."

Angel had mentioned that her friend Jacory was moving in with Tatum and Leona. I hadn't met him.

"She wants to come home, and she's insisting. However, I know that you are her employer and if bringing her home would cause some issue with her employment..."

"No," I interrupted. "Bring her home. Where is her truck?"

"It's at our place. They all rode with me," Jacory explained.

"I'm awake. Bring her home."

"We will be there – if you have to throw up lean out the window, Tatum! – in about fifteen minutes," he finished.

About twenty minutes later, I heard a car pull into the driveway. I opened the door to assist with Angel if needed.

A tall, fair-skinned guy got out of the driver's side of an Infiniti SUV and opened one of the back doors. I saw one of Angel's white pumps slowly hit the pavement, then the other one.

I closely watched his hand placement as he walked her to the front door. Angel was smiling and needed a little assistance, but she seemed ok.

"Mr. Northcott?" he said.

"Yes, it's Xander."

"Xander, I'm Jacory." He extended his hand, and we shook. "Angel and I have known each other for years. Like I said, she had a few drinks, but I watched them the whole night."

"Cory, this is who I was telling you about, Xander, he is one of my most favorite people. He lets me live here and everything! Xander, this is Jacory. He just moved back here from..." Angel slightly slurred.

"The west coast," Jacory finished.

"The west coast," Angel said, then used her pointer finger to tap the tip of Jacory's nose. "Boop."

Jacory winced. "She knows I hate that."

Angel chuckled, which made me smile. I'd never seen her so carefree.

"Are you sure this is okay?" Jacory asked.

"It's her weekend off. She can do whatever makes her happy. It's not a problem. Thanks for bringing her home."

"See, Cory, I told you he was cool. He's also handsome, sexy, and..."

"Okay, Angel," Jacory cut her off as he passed her to me. "These are her keys and her purse. Her phone is in her purse."

"Thank you."

"I will call you tomorrow, Angel," Jacory said.

"You better!" Angel said.

I closed the door behind me and helped Angel down the hall to her bedroom.

"Xander! Hi! I was out having fun with my friends and I think those shots were a little strong," she said while using her thumb and first finger to show the measurement.

"Yeah, it looks like you had a lot of fun," I said while sitting her on her bed.

I went into the bathroom where I'd seen her pajamas and robe hanging. I grabbed those and her bonnet.

"Let's get you changed so you can get in the bed, Angel."

She stood and quickly lifted her dress over her head, exposing her matching black panties and bra. The lace on the bra was thin enough to give me a peek at her dark areolas.

"No, Angel!" I said, quickly pulling her dress back down.

Damn. Her body was perfect.

"You don't want me to put my pajamas on?" Angel tilted her head.

"I do, just – how about this, I will step out while you put on your pajamas. Can you do that for me?"

"I most certainly can. You wanna know why? 'Cause you, Alexander Northcott, are one of my most favorite people."

"You're one of my most favorite people too, Angel. I am going to stand right on the other side of the door."

"Got it!" she said.

I took a deep breath once I stepped out of the room. Angel's body in her bra and panties kept replaying in my mind. Although it was a brief second, I was rock hard and had no idea what to do with myself. I tried to think of other things to get soft, but all I could see was that beautiful bronze skin that looked like it glistened with that black lace on top of it.

Whew.

"All dressed!" Angel announced.

I peeked into the room to make sure she was dressed before opening the door completely. After taking the hairpins out of Angel's bun, I tucked her hair into the oversized bonnet she wore.

"Okay, all done. Go ahead and get in the bed. I will go and grab you some aspirin and Gatorade.

She wrapped her arms around my neck as I was trying to help her into the bed. The next thing I knew, her lips were on mine. Her lips were so soft and sweet. She touched the seam of my lips with her tongue and I let her in. Then I realized what I was doing and quickly pulled away.

"Good night, Angel."

"Good night, Xander," she said.

*A*ngel

"Geezuz," I said after lifting my head from the pillow. I felt a wave of nausea hit me like a freight train. I put my head back down.

Reaching for my phone, I realized it wasn't on the nightstand where I usually put it. I slowly sat up and looked around.

"Wait, when did I get home?" I asked out loud.

I looked at my pajamas then felt for my bonnet.

"What in the world?" I said, scratching my head.

I walked to the bathroom and looked at myself in the mirror, trying to remember last night's events. What I knew for sure was that I was supposed to be at Tatum and Leona's house.

After using the bathroom and brushing my teeth, I went in search of my cell phone. I found my purse on top of my neatly folded dress. Several text notifications popped up once I unlocked my phone.

Tatum: Girl! Where you at? How did you end up at home?

Leona: We kicked it last night! I wish I could remember it.

Angel: I just woke up. I have about 10% of my memory from last night but what I can remember was fun! Why am I home?

Tatum: Jacory said you insisted on going home.

Angel: OMG what did Xander say?

Tatum: Cory said Xander said you were grown and could have as much fun as you wanted. He said he would take care of you.

Tatum: So did he take care of you? (water emoji) (tongue out emoji)

Leona: (eyeballs emoji)

Angel: Let me check my hymen... Nope it's still intact! LOL!

Tatum: (crying laughing emoji)

Leona: (Rolling laughing emoji)

Angel: Tell Cory thank you. I need to go and find Xander. I woke up in my pajamas and with my bonnet on.

Leona: Awww...

Tatum: That's so sweet. Let us know what he says.

Angel: I will.

Slowly peeling my door open, I looked out the door in both directions to see if Xander was in the hall. He wasn't. Mustering up all the courage I had, I stepped out into the hall and went in search of him.

"Xander," I said just above a whisper when I found him sitting in his office staring out the window.

"Good morning," he replied.

His expression gave nothing away. I wasn't sure what his mood was.

"Good morning. Where is Man?" I asked.

"He just went down for a nap. Come in. I need to talk to you," Xander said, causing my stomach to drop like I was experiencing the first drop on a roller coaster. I sat down in one of the chairs in the office.

"I'm so sorry about last night. I don't know why I insisted on coming home or why Cory didn't just take me back to their place. I never drink, so it won't ever happen again, but if it was too much, especially with Man here, then I understand. I can start looking for other employment," I said, all in one breath.

"Whoa," Xander said with his hands in the air. He leaned on the corner of his desk. "Calm down with all that. Jacory called before he brought you here. This is your home. It's not like you were working. You were out enjoying yourself. You can always come home, Angel."

The sincerity in his voice and his calm delivery forced me to take a deep breath and relax back in the chair.

"Really?"

"I enjoyed seeing the carefree Angel. I'm glad you had a good time," Xander said.

"Thank you for helping me. I don't remember putting on my pajamas, this bonnet, or the aspirin by the bed," I admitted.

"That's what I need to talk to you about." Xander ran his hands down the front of his sweatpants then pushed away from the desk to a standing position.

My anxiety returned tenfold. A fluttery feeling in my stomach started. I sat up straight.

"Last night after you came home, we...kissed. More accurately, you kissed me, but I didn't stop it immediately. I did stop you, but – it wasn't immediate. I'm sorry for allowing that to happen. I knew you were inebriated. It was not my intention to ever make you feel uncomfortable around me, and I would never take advantage of you. I would understand if this would affect you wanting to continue working here. Still, I'm not some guy who's trying to sexually harass you or anything like that. So, I'm sorry, Angel. I made sure to get you into your bed after that, and I left your room," Xander explained.

My hand rushed to cover my mouth that had involuntarily fallen open.

"So," I said with a shaky voice, "That wasn't a dream? I really did kiss you last night?"

"You remember?" Xander asked.

"I said something like you're my most favorite person and I kissed you," I recounted.

He nodded.

"Xander! I am so sorry! Oh my gawd. This is so crazy! You shouldn't be the one apologizing; I should be! Oh gawd..." I put my face in my hands.

I was mortified. It had been years since I was so drunk that I couldn't remember things. I hated not being in control. Last night's drinks just snuck up on me. I couldn't believe I'd done something so dumb as kissing Xander.

"Angel, no, it's okay." I felt his hands on my wrists attempting to pry my hands from my embarrassed face. I dropped my hands but wouldn't look at him. He'd stooped down in front of me. "Look at me, Angel."

I slowly looked from the ground into his eyes.

"I didn't want you to have a flashback or something and think that I was trying to be slick since you had been drinking. Which, by the way, drinking and enjoying yourself is totally fine with me."

"I shouldn't have done that! I'm so embarrassed," I responded.

"Don't be embarrassed. The kiss was actually nice. It was brief, but it was nice," Xander replied in a soft tone.

"Really?" I whispered, looking into his eyes. "I remember it being nice, too."

"I like you, Angel."

He moved closer and my breath hitched in my throat while my heart started beating out of my chest.

"I've been trying to come up with a way to tell you for quite some time. I knew I wanted to be with you the day I met you, and that night after Man and I arrived home from the airport, I couldn't get you out of my head. I kicked myself for not getting your last name so I could find you."

"You were with Emmaline."

"Which is why I didn't say anything. Being with her didn't stop me from wanting to be with you, but I knew I couldn't act on those feelings. Emmaline never had my heart, and I knew that for sure, because you captured it during our first encounter. If I'm being too forward or making you uncomfortable, please let me know. I will stop and never speak of it again," Xander said.

"No!" I responded quickly. "I like you too, Xander – a lot."

"Really?" His tentative smile blossomed into a full smile.

"Yes, so what do we do this information?" I asked.

"Well, first, we should..."

His sentence was interrupted by a buzz indicating someone was requesting access through the security gate.

"One sec," he said and stood to look at the security camera.

His face lit up with recognition.

"Mom!" he spoke into the intercom system.

"We forgot the code, baby. Let us in!" his mother responded.

He pressed a button giving them access.

"It's my parents," he smiled. "Can we finish this discussion later?"

"Of course."

I turned to walk away, but he grabbed me by my wrist and pulled me close to him. His lips met mine, and immediately I knew I didn't want to be anywhere else. The kiss wasn't rushed even though his parents would make their way into the house at any moment. He kissed me slowly and deliberately.

He stepped back and looked at me. I blinked a little, trying to get my bearings.

"We'll talk later?" he asked.

"Yes." I smiled. "And thank you for telling me what happened."

"I'll never lie to you or keep anything from you, Angel," Xander said.

9

Angel

X ander left his office before I did. It was as if my feet were superglued to the floor.

"Did that just happen or am I still dreaming?" I asked out loud.

How did people usually wake up from dreams? Maybe pinch themselves? I thought before using my thumb and index finger to grab a hunk of flesh on my arm.

"Ouch!"

I was definitely awake. I couldn't believe Xander liked me. I smiled before I left the office to follow the loud talking.

I stood off to the side, smiling and watching the interaction between Xander and his parents. He and his dad were twins: same chocolate complexion, bushy eyebrows, and a huge smile. Xander had about three inches of height on his dad and Mr. Northcott had about fifty pounds on Xander, but he couldn't deny Xander if he wanted to.

"Xander, you're looking good, son! Fatherhood looks good on you!" Mr. Northcott said.

"Thanks, Dad."

"Xander!" His mother opened her arms for a hug.

Mrs. Northcott was around five-foot-five. She was short compared to the giant men standing next to her. Her jet-black hair was pulled back in a chignon at the nape of her neck. Her tawny skin was smooth and clear and her makeup was flawless. She wore a wrist full of Alex and Ani type bracelets that made a lot of noise when she moved her arm. She was snazzy.

"I missed you, Mom!" Xander said as he hugged his mother.

"I know. I couldn't go another day without seeing you and my grandson. Look who we found along the way." Mrs. Northcott motioned behind her.

"Tati!" Xander yelled. "What are you doing here!"

"What do you mean, what am I doing here? I'm here to see you and my nephew!" Tatiana responded.

They hugged for at least a minute. I'd gotten used to the dad, friend, and boss Xander. I'd never seen the brother and son Xander. I liked him, too.

"Ummm, who is this gorgeous woman standing over there smiling at us?" Tatiana asked.

Xander turned to me and smiled, which made me smile harder. He took his mother's hand and led her over to me.

"Mom, Dad, Tati, this is Angel. Angel, this is my family," Xander said.

"Hi!" I smiled.

"We hug around here," Mrs. Northcott said as she pulled me in for a hug.

"Nice to meet you in person, darling," Mr. Northcott said.

"Hi, Angel," Tatiana smiled.

"So, where is my grandson?" Mrs. Northcott asked.

"He was asleep, but he's probably waiting for someone to come and get him," Xander said.

"I'll get him," I volunteered.

Xander winked at me right before I turned in the direction of Maximus' room, sending a million butterflies to flight in my stomach.

Sure enough, when I poked my head in the door of Maximus' room, he was looking right at me.

"What are you doing awake, Man? Your daddy just put you down for a nap."

Maximus spit and cooed until I picked him up.

"Your family is here to meet you."

I changed Maximus' diaper and wiped his face before I took him into the living room.

"Oh, my goodness!" Mrs. Northcott said as I walked over to her with Maximus. "Look at him, Vincent. He looks just like Xander when he was a baby."

"Except for this head of hair," Mr. Northcott said, touching Maximus' head.

Maximus was spiting and cooing, soaking up all the attention.

"You are just the most handsome baby, ever," Mrs. Northcott said as she nuzzled Maximus' neck.

He laughed out loud when she did it. I smiled, too. I quietly made my way back into my room to nurse the lingering headache I had from last night.

After swallowing the aspirin on my nightstand and drinking down half a bottle of Gatorade, I sat down on the bed to process what had just happened.

"He actually kissed me..." I whispered to myself.

I smiled while replaying the kiss, recalling the gentle force that he'd used to pull me toward him. The way he possessively wrapped his arm around my waist, resting his hand in the safe spot right above my behind. I licked my lips while remembering how incredible his soft lips felt pressed against mine. Then I moaned a little, reminiscing on the way my stomach fluttered as he sensually and thoroughly kissed me. No one had ever made me feel half of what I'd felt in that brief interaction with Xander.

Navigating to my soul playlist, I plugged my ears with my AirPods and picked up my sketch pad. I didn't want to interfere with Xander and his family getting reacquainted. I knew Maximus was okay and if he needed anything, Xander would let me know.

"Hey," I said after opening the door to my bathroom that separated mine and Maximus' rooms.

"I'm sorry, did I wake you?" Tatiana asked.

"No," I stretched. "I mean, I was asleep, but I must've dozed off."

I had no idea how long I'd been asleep.

"I was about to put Maximus' new clothes and toys away, but I thought maybe you had a system. I didn't want to come in messing things up," Tatiana said.

"Oh, yeah, there is somewhat of a system, but I wouldn't have minded you putting them away."

"Can you show me? It would give me a second to get to know you before my mother comes and finds you."

"Okay," I chuckled and followed her through the bathroom into Maximus' room.

There were several bags of clothes and toys situated near Maximus's closet.

"As you can see, my mother and I went a little overboard," Tatiana said, retrieving the bags.

Tatiana's deep chestnut skin matched Xander's. They shared the same dark eyes and thick eyebrows. Her features were soft, while Xander had hard, masculine features. There was no mistaking they were siblings.

"Well, he's the first baby in the family, and he's super worth it, so..." I smiled and shrugged.

"So, how is this nanny gig going for you?" Tatiana asked.

She began taking the items out of the bags.

"I love it! Maximus and Xander, my two most favorite people."

"But you've never been a nanny before, correct?" she asked.

"I cared for some children when I was in college, but I've had a career since then," I explained.

I took the t-shirts she'd just folded and put them in Maximus' drawer.

"Xan told me about the plane ride and how you helped him care for Maximus."

"He did?"

"Yep, he did. Then he said you were the last person he interviewed for the position," Tatiana further revealed.

"Yeah, that was crazy. I couldn't believe my eyes when I walked into that interview and saw Xander," I replied, grinning.

"So, you remembered him?" Tatiana asked.

"Of course I did."

"Oh..." Tatiana looked at me and smiled. "You like him back?"

"Huh?"

"I've known my brother since the day he was born. I know him better than he knows himself. I saw how he looked at you. Now I see it's mutual," Tatiana said.

I smiled. If that kiss was any indication, then he liked me a lot.

"How do you like living in Austria?" I asked.

"Yeah, I'll go ahead and let you change the subject," she said with a smirk. "It's okay. You don't have to say anything. I'll force him to spill the beans later."

I smiled again.

"I like it there. I miss my brother and my parents, but it's my dream," Tatiana answered.

"I've been to Vienna. I ate at a restaurant that was down the street from the symphony building. What is called?"

"Musikverein," Tatiana responded.

"Right, I remember it sounded something like music to me since I didn't speak a lick of German. I had barbecued beef that was so tender it melted in your mouth. I also ate at an Ethiopian restaurant there. I had shekla tibs. The strips of meat were roasted in a clay pot with hot coals underneath. They served it with some injera, which is a flatbread. I was surprised to find Ethiopian cuisine, but it was so good."

"You sound like my brother. He describes places he's traveled the exact same way; he talks about the food," Tatiana smiled.

"I love food. That's what traveling is about for me, the food."

"I can tell," Tatiana smiled.

"Hey," Xander said after poking his head into the room. "What are you in here doing? Did you wake Angel up?" He looked at Tatiana. "Did she wake you up?" He looked at me.

I shook my head. "No."

He squinted his eyes at Tatiana.

"What? I didn't wake her up! I came in here to put Maximus's things away. But I was just about to tell Angel about the time you encouraged me to cut half my ponytail off," Tatiana responded.

"I did not encourage you!" Xander debated.

"Yes, you did! You said people with long hair cut their hair to sell to other people," Tatiana said.

"So that was the encouragement?" Xander deadpanned.

"You watched me do it and told me to go higher. And you told me Mommy wouldn't notice!" Tatiana laughed.

She and Xander shared the same smile.

"If you don't get out of here telling those," Xander looked behind him then whispered, "lies."

"Lie is a bad word in our household," Tatiana explained.

I laughed, thinking about BG correcting me the one and only time I had used the word in front of her.

"I thought I was the only one who couldn't use it," I chuckled.

"No, Momma doesn't play when it comes to that word," Tatiana said.

"If you're in here telling stories, you should tell her the one when you encouraged me to take Dad's car to 7-eleven to get some nachos talking about he would never know," Xander said.

"You wanted nachos, too!" Tatiana rebutted.

I enjoyed watching them together.

They went back and forth several times over whose fault it was when they scraped the car trying to get it back into the garage

"Anyway," Xander said, "Mom decided to cook and dinner is ready. Angel, are you hungry?"

I'd smelled something cooking and thought it was Chef Perry.

"Yes, I'm starving."

*X*ander

After fixing our plates and Mom saying a quick prayer over the food, we all dug in. Mom made smothered chicken, mashed potatoes, and green beans. It felt like I hadn't eaten her cooking in years. After eating food from renowned chefs worldwide, I was still confident that my mother's cooking was the best I'd ever tasted.

"So, Angel, how do you like being Maximus' caretaker?" Mom questioned.

"I was just telling Tatiana that I love caring for Maximus. He has such an old soul and makes my job very easy," Angel replied with an easy grin.

I loved the way she spoke of Maximus.

"He's special like his dad," Mom said.

"I agree," Angel said softly.

We smiled at each other.

"Xander, have you thought about getting Maximus christened? We could have the ceremony at the church and then a celebration afterwards," Mom asked.

"Uh..." I looked at Tati for help.

She looked down at her plate like she couldn't feel our twinapathy. Then I realized she knew Mom was going to ask me about it.

"I mean, it doesn't have to be anything elaborate..." Mom started.

"Really?" Dad asked with one eyebrow hiked.

"No, Vincent, it doesn't have to be," Mom answered and rolled her eyes.

"Pearl, you know you are going to have ponies and bouncy houses, sword swallowers and tight rope walkers, Xander doesn't want that," Dad responded.

Our mother had the tendency to plan "simple" parties that ended up being the event of the century. Tati and I wanted a small, simple high school graduation party. We got an event large enough for the entire class plus their friends to attend. There was a DJ, photographer, balloon arches, an indoor pool, a local rapper, and a magician. The city council presented us with decrees recognizing our high school graduation. It was the exact opposite of what we'd asked for.

"We don't have to have a party, per se. Maximus should at least be christened, Xan," Mom said.

"I would like to have him christened, but Mom, I don't want a party."

"Not even a small get together with the family so they can all see him?" Mom pleaded.

I looked at Tati.

"He's the first baby in the family, Brother," Tati added.

She'd finally made eye contact with me.

"He should be celebrated," Angel chimed in.

"They got you, too?" I asked Angel.

Angel shrugged.

"I mean, it's the least you could let me do since I didn't get to do anything when Piper passed," Mom said.

"Awww," both Tati and I said at the same time.

"You went low, Mommy. That's not what we agreed on," Tati laughed.

"Fine, Mom. Have at it," I relented.

Dad quietly shook his head.

"Yes!" Mom rubbed her hands together. "You will need to think about godparents."

"I will probably ask Everett and Kerry," I responded.

"Good, I will take care of the rest," Mom said.

"I can't believe you," I mouthed to Tati.

She smiled and shrugged.

"Hey Xan, I picked these up while we were in Cuba," Dad said while holding two cigars. "You want to come out back with me and have one?"

"Of course."

Angel, Mom, and Tati had disappeared into Maximus' room.

I grabbed a bottle of bourbon, two glasses, my cigar clipper, and followed my dad outside. We sat in the Adirondack chairs facing the pool.

While sitting silently enjoying the evening air and our cigars, I thought about how I would approach Angel to finish our conversation. I asked myself if having a non-sexual relationship with Angel would be hard for me; but quickly determined that it would be challenging, but she was worth every single day I would have to wait. I'd promised myself I wouldn't pressure her or dwell on it. I needed her in my life.

"So, how is it going?" Dad asked.

"It's going a lot different than I planned."

"Life will throw you some curveballs," Dad said.

"Absolutely. You know how I felt when Piper first told me she was pregnant. I always wanted a family but not with someone I barely knew. After Piper and I agreed on our parenting arrangement, I was okay with having Maximus on holidays and summers once he was old enough to travel. When the nurse put him in my arms, I immediately rethought all the custody stuff Piper and I had agreed on. I quickly thought about moving to California, so I could see him every day. I even thought about trying to establish a romantic relationship with Piper to be close to him. All of that passed through my mind in seconds. I didn't want to put him down. It was like my heart expanded, and I knew what real love was. I knew I would love that lil' dude forever, no matter what."

"I remember when you were born. Watching your mother go through all that pain. Feeling completely and utterly helpless to stop it. Then seeing your little face. It made every decision I'd made to get to that point worth it. I had a son, someone who would carry my name and bloodline on for another generation. As soon as I settled in with you, the doctor and nurses started scrambling, talking about it's another one. After your sister was born, I promised myself that I would be the best man I could for the both of you. I ain't gone lie, though. Fatherhood can be tough," Dad finished.

"Fatherhood is already tough and scary. How do you manage? Who did you look to for advice?"

"I looked to my dad for some advice, but I realized he was limited to his experiences. He was a good source, but I needed more. That's when I started going to church with your mother. I wasn't a religious man, but I knew I needed God's help if I was going to live up to the promise that I made to be the best man I could," Dad said.

"Yeah, you and leaning on something bigger than all of us is my plan as well. Also, I'm much more intentional with my decisions and actions like I've been reconsidering opening my own restaurant."

"Oh yeah?"

"Yeah, I looked over my old business plan for Ethos. When I initially thought about opening it and started taking steps to get it started, I got promoted from the kitchen. I thought I was satisfied not being in the kitchen, but I miss it. Angel saw the business plan on my desk the other day and got so excited when I told her about it. She encouraged me to pursue it."

"Miss Angel seems to be an important piece of the puzzle around here. Is she more than just the nanny? What does Emmaline think of her?"

"Emma and I are over for good."

"Oh yeah?" Dad smiled.

"Yeah, she had a hard time adjusting to the idea of Maximus and an even harder time adjusting to Angel. Neither of them is going anywhere. So, that's dead and buried. Never to be resurrected again. I care for Angel. I care for her more than I've ever cared for a woman. Without trying, she makes my house feel like a home with fresh flowers and music. I look forward to coming home to her and Maximus. Maximus loves her and she loves him. Of course, I kept my distance while I was still with Emma, but I finally found the right words to tell her how I felt right before you arrived. Like as soon as I got the first few sentences out, you guys were at the gate."

"Aww, bad timing," Dad laughed.

"Awful timing," I laughed. "I want to explore something with Angel, though."

"I like her. In the short time we've been around her, she seems genuine. Did you find her through an agency?" Dad asked.

"Yes, but I guess I haven't had a chance to tell you how we really met. I was on the plane coming home after Piper passed..."

*A*ngel

After Mrs. Northcott and Tati helped me bathe Man, Mrs. Northcott insisted that she give him his bottle and put him down since it was my day off. I didn't mind allowing her to spend as much time with Maximus as she wanted. I kissed Maximus and went back into my room.

While listening to my old school jazz station, I mindlessly sketched while thinking about the conversation Xander and I needed to have.

Was it silly of me to catch feelings for my employer? Didn't people have workplace romances all the time? But did they end well? If we were to date, what would that look like? Was it a good idea to date someone you lived with? I wondered if he would be okay with waiting until I was ready for sex. How long was too long? Was I ready for sex? I'd thought about it a lot more in the past few months than I ever had.

"Hey?"

I jumped when I looked up and saw Xander standing in front of me.

"Oh my gawd!" I yelped.

"I didn't mean to scare you," he chuckled. "I knocked, but you didn't answer. I heard the music playing and figured you'd fallen asleep. I was coming in to turn the music off for you."

Applying slight pressure to my chest with my hand, trying to get my heart to slow down from the sudden rush of adrenaline, I took a deep breath.

"I didn't hear you come in. I guess I was lost in my thoughts."

"I'll leave if I'm disturbing you."

"No, please stay."

I moved over on the small couch, giving him space to sit down.

"You are working on a new chocolate design?" he asked, motioning toward my sketch pad.

"I have no idea what I was trying to do," I chuckled after looking at the random doodling on the paper.

"Mom wants to have a cookout tomorrow. She hasn't seen Everett, Kerry, and his family in a while. I have a couple other friends I invited. I was wondering if you wanted to invite your friends. Also, Garrett, if it's not too late. I wanted to have some time to discuss his farm and using his services."

"Really?"

"Yes, I am going to start moving forward with Ethos."

"That is amazing, Xander! I am so happy and excited for you. Ethos is going to be a game-changer."

"I think it will be too. Thanks for the encouragement."

"Of course. I will text everyone right now. I know Leona, Tatum, and Jacory will be here with bells on. They love free food. Tatum has talked about your pool since I moved in."

"Well, tell them to bring suits. We will eat and enjoy the outdoors," Xander said.

I quickly sent two text messages, then tucked my phone away.

"I have something else I wanted to discuss with you, and we need to finish our conversation from earlier if you're down for that?" Xander said.

"Sure," I responded.

"So, you know I agreed to have Man christened?"

"Yes, christening is a huge thing where I come from. All my little cousins were christened at BG and Papa's church."

"Yeah and I figured mom would ask about it. So I've been thinking, and I'm going to ask Everett and Kerry to be Man's godparents," Xander said.

"That's a great choice."

"And," he took my hand in his before continuing, "it would be my honor if you would also be Man's godmother."

I froze.

"I mean, you represent everything that a mother is to him. He probably thinks of you as his mom. If something happened to me, I wouldn't want him to be on this earth without you. Am I asking too much?" Xander finished.

I swallowed to clear the lump in my throat.

"Xander, it would be my honor to be Man's godmother. I can't think of anything else that would bring me more pleasure or satisfaction in this whole world. Thank you for thinking of me."

He pulled me in for a hug. Being in his arms felt like the best, most secure place on earth.

"And about our conversation earlier," he started after we separated. "If I learned nothing else from Piper's death, I learned that time is precious. When you want something or know something to be right for you, you have to go after it. Although it took me a minute to say this to you, I'm telling you now; I want to be your man. I want you to be my lady. I know where you are with sex, and I will wait and never rush you or put any pressure on you. It's not an end goal for me. You in my life forever is the end goal for me. From the second I met you, you changed me. I don't want to be without you."

"No one has ever said such beautiful words to me. I have found security and a place to rest with you. You've allowed me to... just be. No pressure. No rushing. Your calm demeanor and confidence have made me stronger. Hell yeah, I want to be your girl."

He moved in to kiss me. This time I was ready. I anticipated the feel of his silky, moist lips on top of mine.

In a slow, unhurried pace, he placed his lips against mine and said, "You're are gorgeous, Angelica."

I felt a gush of fluid in my panties. He had barely touched me and I'd completely ruined my underwear.

I moaned as he placed delicate kisses down my neck to my collarbone and back up again. With every kiss, the warmth in my body increased. I grabbed his neck and possessively captured his lips, requesting immediate access into his mouth.

He made a throaty sound as I played with his tongue while kissing him. I kept my grip on the back of his neck while we continued to kiss. I reluctantly let him go remembering that there were other people in the house.

We kissed, talked, and listened to music well into the night. I fell asleep in his arms.

Xander

"So," Tatiana said after waking me up by putting her wet finger in my ear.

"So, what?" I said, looking at my clock that read six in the morning. "Why are you torturing me so early in the morning?"

I'd stayed in Angel's room most of the night. We both fell asleep. I woke up and went into my room after tucking her in.

"Jet lag," she shrugged. "Momma must have it too because she already sent Angel back to bed volunteering to take care of Maximus."

"This isn't her day to work, so I'm sure she didn't mind."

"Nope, she directed Mommy to where everything was and went back into her room. So, you like her, huh?"

"Why are you in my business, little girl?"

"Why wouldn't I be? I have absolutely no business of my own, so while I'm here, I might as well be all up in and through yours," she chuckled.

I sat up in my bed.

"She told me she is a chef. How does a chef become a nanny?" Tatiana asked.

"She was taking a break from the kitchen."

"Oh, so y'all have that in common, too?" Tatiana sassed.

Tatiana didn't like the idea of me leaving the kitchen and becoming the Vice President of Operations.

"You know this job morphed into what it is now. I thought I would have more time in the kitchen."

"Whatever, that silly ass Emmaline encouraged you to move that way because she had no idea that food was your passion."

"I can admit that I miss the kitchen, which is why I've been considering Ethos again."

"Eek!" Tatiana shrieked. "You're really gonna do it this time?"

"You think it's a good idea?"

"What! Are you shitting me? Of course, it's a magnificent idea!" Tatiana said.

"Angel introduced me to a farmer who would be willing to partner with me on the farm to table menu. I spoke to two of my chef friends, and they both are willing to do guest spots. I mean, it won't happen tomorrow, but it can happen."

"Brother... I like her for you even though you haven't confirmed that you like her. She had the house smelling all good. The garden looks great. She takes care of Maximus like she birthed him, and she's encouraging you to follow your dreams? And – remember what you told me when you finally broke up with Eviline the first time?"

"What?"

"You said you wanted to be with someone who understood your drive and your hustle. You wanted someone you could talk shop with and dream with," Tati quoted.

"What are you? A recorder?"

"No, but I remembered you said that because I started to specifically pray that way for you. I'm all the way on the other side of the world and I don't want you here by yourself."

I did remember saying those words. It was before I'd met Piper. That was probably why I was so drawn to Angel. She was everything I'd said I wanted.

"I do like her a lot. I told her last night," I confessed.

"What did she say?"

"She said she liked me, too."

"I knew it!" Tati slapped her hand on the bed. "Wait!" she jumped up from the bed and looked at the sheets.

"You're stupid!" I laughed. "Nothing happened on these sheets."

"I was about to say," Tati laughed and climbed back in the bed.

I climbed out of bed and went to the restroom. I heard someone knock on the door.

"Come in," Tati yelled.

"Oh, I'm sorry," I heard Angel say.

"It's okay, come in. We're starting the party early," I heard Tati respond.

I quickly spat out the toothpaste in my mouth and shouted, "Give me one sec."

After wiping my face, I grabbed a clean t-shirt and threw it on.

I found Angel and Tati giggling about something. Angel turned to me and smiled. My chest filled with air knowing that she was finally mine.

"What?" I asked.

"It's just girl stuff. I'm going to go and make sure Momma hasn't invited the whole town of St. Helane to dinner today. You know they would drive the two and a half hours just to eat some free food," Tati laughed.

She left and closed the door behind her. I walked over to Angel and put my arms around her waist, pulling her closer to me. She smelled amazing.

"Good morning," I said before placing a quick kiss on her lips.

"Good morning," she smiled.

"What's up?"

I led her to the balcony and sat down in the chair. I pulled her onto my lap.

"My friends are so hyped about coming over here to swim and eat," she chuckled. "What do you want me to tell them to bring?"

"Nothing. I'm sure mom has it all covered."

"Naw, they ignant. They need rules and boundaries or you will never get rid of them. They're like feral cats. Feed 'em once they keep coming back," Angel chuckled.

"Okay, tell them to bring drinks."

She quickly typed out something on her phone.

"See," she chuckled, showing me the response to her text.

Leona: Black people drinks or name brand drinks?

Tatum: Right, like do we bring Shasta and Stars & Stripes or Coke-Cola and Pepsi?

Jacory: What is Stars & Stripes?

Leona: You know, from the Dollar Tree

Jacory: Oh that was the shit in college. The orange flavor?

Leona: Yeah we all had headaches from the artificial sweetener in it but it was cheap and good.

Tatum: Do y'all have Styrofoam plates and aluminum foil?

Jacory: Don't be over there using up their foil. We can pull off a couple sheets from the roll we just bought.

I laughed.

"They sound like my friends."

"But they are all in the same house! This is ridiculous!" she laughed.

"That Stars & Stripes will give you a headache, though," I agreed.

"I know, but when we were in college, we threw plenty of parties with some Mountain, Cola, and Orange Stars & Stripes," she laughed.

She typed out something else on her phone then tucked it in her pocket.

"Oh and Garrett is coming. He's bringing some fresh vegetables and rum," Angel said.

"That rum is excellent."

"I know. He doesn't always have it, so when he does, I'm always trying to get a couple bottles of it," she explained.

"Do your friends know you're my girl?"

"No, I will tell them when they come over today. They won't be surprised, though. Tatum called it a while ago."

"Really?"

"Yeah, she figured out that I would fall for you," Angel said.

"Fall? Is that what has happened?"

"Definitely," she said, then turned her body to straddle my lap. "Is that not a good word?"

She kissed my neck right behind my ear. I knew she felt my dick come alive because she lightly moved her warm core against it. I tightly gripped each side of the chair.

"Xander," she whispered her lips against my ear. "Is that not a good word?"

She moved her hips.

"It's a great word," I responded, enjoying the feeling of her on top of me. I tightened my grip on the chair as she continued to kiss and nibble on my neck.

"Xander," she whispered again.

"Mmmhmm," I responded.

"I'm a virgin, but I'm not naïve to intimacy. I want you – no, I *need* you to touch me."

"I don't want you to feel rushed or uncomfortable," I explained.

"Your touch will never make me feel either one of those things, touch me," she whispered as she rocked against my hardness.

I slid my hands into the shorts she wore past the elastic waistband and grabbed two handfuls of her ass and pressed her center into mine.

She moaned and a surge of electricity shot through me. Her soft hands gently placed on either side of my face was a stark contrast to the way she forcefully and hungrily kissed me. I granted every access she requested. When she slid her tongue across my lips, I opened my mouth. She peppered kisses across my face and down my neck. I stretched my neck, giving her more areas to explore. She was in control and I loved every minute of it.

I grabbed her tightly to keep her in place. I could feel the tension building up in my stomach.

"Whoa, it's about to be a mess," I warned.

"We can clean it up," she said against my lips and continued to rock her hips.

I held onto her ass, feeling myself about to come.

"It's so hard," she moaned.

"You're so soft," I responded.

She moaned as I moved one of my hands under her shirt and rolled her hardened nipple between my thumb and forefinger.

"Ahh," she said and threw her head back. She sucked her bottom lip into her mouth and her movements stalled just as I climaxed.

She collapsed on my chest.

"Are you okay?" I asked while rubbing her back.

"Yes, I'm perfect," she said.

*A*ngel
      The impromptu barbeque was in full swing. All my friends had arrived and were loving the pool. I kept having flashbacks to my and Xander's makeout session. Every time I thought about it, I had to do Kegel exercises to relieve some of the pressure between my thighs.

Garrett arrived and had an assortment of fresh vegetables that we washed and sent out to Mr. Northcott to be placed on the grill. Xander made a ridiculously delicious seafood macaroni. I made several trays of rum bonbons and a gooey butter cake. Mrs. Northcott made all the rest of the sides.

Mr. Northcott was in his element on the grill. With a beer in his hand and tongs in the other, Jacory kept him company. Tati was in the pool watching Maximus in his floaty device while laughing and talking with Leona and Tatum. Doctor Everett and his wife Kerry came with their two children, and Chef Perry and his family came. Several of Xander's cousins were in attendance as well.

"Did I tell you how amazing you look in this swimming suit, Angelica?" Xander said into my ear from behind.

I loved the way my full name sounded coming from his mouth. I popped the last batch of rum chocolates out of the mold and turned around to face him. He placed his hands on the island on both sides of me, pinning me in.

"Yes, but I don't mind hearing it again," I said.

"If I knew you would wear this to a pool party, I would've thrown one as soon as you moved in," Xander said.

"If you would've thrown a party when I first moved in, I wouldn't have worn this one. I have a yellow one that would've gotten your attention."

"Oh yeah?" he said into my neck.

"Mmmhmm," I moaned, not caring that we had a whole house of people.

"How about this, I will throw a private pool party, just for you and me. Will you wear the yellow one then?"

"Why would I wear anything to a party with just me and you?"

"Angelica," he huffed.

"Alexander," I replied in the same tone.

"Don't play with me. I will kick all these people out of my house right now, including my mother and Maximus."

"Aye, Xander," Everett said after entering the kitchen.

"Neeegggrrrooo..." Xander stretched out the word.

"My bad," Everett threw his hands up in surrender. "I didn't know you were in here having a private moment. Aye, now you know how it felt when you bust in on me when we were in the freshman dorms, and I was mid..."

Kerry walked into the kitchen. I watched Xander do a quick nod and look behind Everett.

Everett took notice because he quickly changed the story, "You bust in on me while I was in the middle of studying..."

"No, please continue with the original story. You were about to talk about some little girl in college," Kerry said.

"Huh," Everett said.

"Girl? I thought you were about to tell the story about the all-day study session I walked in on," Xander said.

"See, you have to watch these two," Kerry laughed.

"I have no idea what you are referring to," Xander smiled.

"Baby, you know you're my first, my last, my everything," Everett said while hugging Kerry.

She rolled her eyes but settled into the hug.

"Pops told me to come in here and get you so you can get obliterated on this bones table. What's his name, the big guy with the deep voice that reminds me of John Coffey from *The Green Mile*?" Everett said.

"Garrett," I chuckled.

When I'd first met him, he did remind me of a lighter, prettier version of John Coffey. His bald head, deep voice, and denim overalls did it for me. I guess even without the denim overalls, he still reminded people of the character.

"Yeah, aye, he's interesting. He was talking about black people and farms and crap. I was enthralled. Anyway, he's playing and that pretty muthfucka..." Everett started.

"Why don't you know anybody's name?" Kerry interrupted.

"I don't know. I forget as soon as they tell me. But you know the one that works in tech," Everett finished.

"Cory?"

"Yeah, they all out there talking all crap about how well they play. So, let's go run this table," Everett said.

"I came in here to get some more of these pretty chocolates before they are all inhaled like the last batch. They are almost too pretty to eat," Kerry said.

"Thank you," I replied, still pinned to the island. "Take as many as you want."

"Alright, here I come," Xander said.

Both Kerry and Everett grabbed several chocolates before they left the kitchen.

"It looks like I have a private party to plan," Xander said.

"Let me know when. I'll be there," I shot back with a wink.

⠿⠿⠿ ⠀⠀ ⠿⠿⠿ ⠀⠀ ⠿⠿⠿

*A*fter the party was over, most of the guests left. My friends stayed behind to help clean up. Mrs. Northcott made sure to fix all three of them substantial to-go plates, which automatically endeared her to them forever.

"The party was really nice," Leona said.

We'd settled around the fire pit after we cleaned the house and the backyard. I was feeding Man his last bottle before bedtime. It felt like I hadn't spent much time with him in the previous few days, but there was plenty of help with his family in town. Mrs. Northcott had already told me that she would put him down since I was still entertaining.

"We did have fun," Tatum added.

"Can I join y'all?" Tatiana asked.

"Of course."

We all adjusted our chairs so she could fit in.

"So, Tatiana, when are you going back to Vienna?" Leona asked.

"Well, I had taken a leave of absence thinking my brother needed me but just wasn't saying anything. But boy was I wrong," Tatiana looked at me.

Everyone laughed.

"She's holding it down over here, right?" Tatum said.

"Girl, when my brother is not smiling from ear to ear, he is following her around the room with his eyes," Tatiana said.

"I know, right?" Tatum said.

"You guys make a cute couple," Leona smiled. "You smile as much as he does."

He did make me smile.

Earlier in the day I told all three of my friends about mine and Xander's newly cemented relationship status. They were all happy. Jacory even gave his blessing. He'd never liked any guy that was interested in us.

"I am probably going to stay through the christening then head back. The director was very understanding. He has a twin as well," Tatiana explained.

"Will the christening be here?" Leona asked.

"No, it will be down in St. Helane, where my parents live. I'm sure my mother is going to invite all of you. So be prepared for an over the top extravaganza even though she told Xander that she wouldn't," Tatiana laughed.

"When we find out the dates, I will ask my real estate contacts about a corporate rental we can all stay in down there," Leona said.

"Yeah, let's make a weekend of it," Tatum said.

"If y'all come, see if Garrett wants to come to," Tatiana said.

"Okay?" Tatum said. "That is one hunk of a man!"

"I wonder if all of him is hunky," Tatiana said.

"It won't hurt to find out," Tatum said.

"It might, but I won't complain," Tatiana said.

We all laughed.

"What are y'all laughing at?" Xander said after walking over with Jacory.

"Nothing!" Tatiana said.

We all laughed again.

"Whatever," Xander said and pulled Tatiana's hair.

"Oww, stop weirdo!" Tatiana laughed.

"Babe..."

My heart skipped. Was he calling me babe?

"Mom is going to put Man down if he's finished with his bottle," Xander said.

"Okay," I smiled.

I thought I'd liked it when he called me Angelica but I liked it even more when he called me babe.

10

Xander

$\mathcal{W}$e had a huge catering event to prepare for at one of the restaurants, so I'd worked a little later than I planned. Tatiana had spent the day out visiting with some old friends. Mom and Dad had taken Man to see some of their friends around town.

Angel and I usually sent messages all day, but I was so busy, we didn't send many, and the messages she did send were short. I could tell she wasn't feeling well.

I tapped on Angel's bathroom door before I entered her room.

"Come in," I heard her say faintly.

The room was dark except for the light from the full moon shining through her open window.

She had her back to me, but I could tell from her slumped shoulders and her head resting on her folded arms that she was not in a good mood. Plus, there was no music playing.

"What's going on?" I asked.

She turned to me, and immediately I noticed her red, swollen eyes and the speckles of tissue on her face that had been left behind after she'd tried to wipe her face.

"Angel, did something happen?"

I sat down next to her and mentally prepared myself for something devastating, although I knew it had nothing to do with Man or my family because I'd just spoken to my family and checked in on a sleeping Man before I entered her room. Hopefully, her whole family was well.

Her big beautiful eyes welled up with tears, the corners of her mouth lowered, and she began to cry. I pulled her close to me, not knowing what was happening but hoping that my presence helped some.

"Papa's birthday is tomorrow. I'm not home to go and place some flowers on his grave or something. Once again, I'm not there when I should be," she cried.

I had no idea how it felt to lose a grandparent. All my grandparents were still alive. I even had a step-grandfather. I had no way of fixing her pain, so I just let her cry and held her until she stopped.

"Would you like me to find a ticket so you can go home and spend some time with your grandmother and mother?"

"No, BG said don't come back for that, and Mom is out on the road with some band," she answered.

I went into her bathroom and wet a washcloth with warm water. I used the towel to wipe away the tissue residue on her face.

"What can I do?" I asked sincerely. I had no idea, but I wanted to try to make it better.

"Hold me," she responded.

I quickly kicked off my shoes and climbed into her bed. She laid down next to me and rested her head on my chest. I rubbed her back until she fell asleep.

⁂

"Come in," Angel said after I lightly tapped on her door.

She appeared to be in better spirits than she had been the night before, but I knew today would be a hard day for her.

"Hey, I know it's last minute, but can you go somewhere with me in about an hour? It's an all-white affair but not too dressy because it's at the bluffs."

"Umm..." She looked around, probably trying to figure out an excuse not to go.

"My mother and father will watch Man," I added.

"Okay, I have a white dress and some sandals I can put on. I should be ready in an hour," she relented.

"Okay."

I went into my room and sent a couple text messages before I changed into my distressed white jeans, a white button-down shirt and my Gucci sneakers.

I didn't have to wait long for Angel to emerge from her room wearing a white blouse that rested low on her shoulders and a long white skirt to match. The long split in front of the skirt showed her shapely leg every time she took a step. She carried a small white bag and had on flat white sandals.

"All white was made specifically for you, gorgeous."

"Thank you," she replied smiling.

I took her hand, interlocked our fingers, and led her to the truck.

She was not her usual talkative self. She mostly stared out her window. I caught her wiping a couple tears away as we drove past Central Market. I'm sure seeing all the restaurants sparked some memories of her grandfather.

After the forty-five-minute drive, we arrived at Cornelius Bluff, one of the highest bluffs in Sable Falls. Angel perked up when she saw all the white balloons and her friends and my family in all white waiting on us.

"What is this?" Angel asked, looking back at her friends while I parked the truck.

"This is a memorial in honor of Chef Quincy Saint Rose," I announced.

I'd gotten up early and made quick plans for an impromptu memorial ceremony for Angel's grandfather. She listed her grandmother's number as her emergency contact on her employee information sheet, so I was able to get a picture of Chef Saint Rose that Leona took and got a sizeable physical print of and placed it in a nice frame on an easel. Tatum purchased white balloons for everyone to release. My mother thought it would be an excellent idea for Angel to release a butterfly. I was impressed by how fast these women put this together for me. I gave them my idea and they all ran with it.

I walked around, opened Angel's door, and helped her out the truck.

"What are you talking about?" she asked.

"We wanted you to have something here since you couldn't go back to California," I explained.

My sister sat in a white folding chair in her all-white and played music on the violin as we approached.

My mother had even dressed Man in an all-white outfit. He was content in his stroller.

"Oh Papa," Angel cried when she saw the picture of her grandfather resting on the easel. "Where did this picture come from?"

Chef Saint Rose looked regal in his black chef smock and hat with his arms folded in front of him.

"BG sent it," Tatum smiled.

Leona handed everyone a white balloon before my father spoke.

"I didn't have the pleasure of meeting your grandfather, Angel. That's my loss, but I have experienced the seed that he planted in you. So, through you, I know him. I know that he loved people. I know that his light shone brightly and that his culinary talent was not matched. How do I know? Because you are the same way. Some people leave this earth and don't leave anything behind, but your grandfather left a legacy— you," Dad finished.

Everyone wiped tears.

"Today, we honor Chef Saint Rose on his birthday and release this butterfly into the world as a memorial of his transition to be with his Heavenly Father. Continue to rest on Chef Saint Rose and happy heavenly birthday," my mother said.

Mom handed Angel a small box. Angel opened it and a beautiful monarch butterfly flew out and away.

Tatiana began to play "I Put a Spell on You" by Nina Simone, one of Chef Saint Rose's favorite musicians.

I'd almost forgotten how magnificent Tati was on the violin.

Leona came and held Angel's other hand through the duration of the song.

"Would you like to say something before we release the balloons?" I asked Angel.

She nodded as she wiped her tears.

"Umm," Angel started. "I've dreaded this day for months. Papa was my grandfather, protector, confidant, cheerleader, and teacher. I never imagined my life without him. When he died, I felt like he took a piece of me with him, not a piece actually, but a huge chunk. He taught me loyalty, commitment, survival, and tenacity. He didn't care that I was a black woman in a white male-dominated industry. He told me to go in there and make them remember me through my food. He said, don't talk a lot. Just show then who you are. That's what I did. That's what I was doing when he died. So, I honor you, Papa, today, and every day as I live the unapologetic life you taught me to live. I love you. Happy birthday."

"Happy birthday," we all repeated.

Tati played "Contemplation" by McCoy Tyner as we released the balloons into the air and watched them float away.

*A*ngel
I cried so much at Papa's memorial, I almost felt dehydrated. I would've never expected that they would put something like that together for me.

"Thank you so much," I said after hugging Mr. Northcott.

"No thanks necessary, darlin'," he responded.

"The butterfly was beautiful," I told Mrs. Northcott.

"I know how hard it is to lose someone you love. We are here to support you, sweetheart," she responded.

"Man!" I said, bending down to check out his all-white outfit. "You didn't tell me they were surprising me!"

He smiled and spoke some gibberish before he started blowing spit bubbles.

"We are going to take him back home with us if that's okay?" Mrs. Northcott said.

"Go ahead, Mom. We will be back later," Xander answered.

I kissed Man before they headed to their car.

I hugged Tatiana. "Thank you. That was beautiful. You made me cry harder!"

"You're welcome. Now you know why they got a bitch all up in another country," she cracked with a smile.

"I do!" I laughed.

"I'm going back with Mom and Dad," Tatiana said.

"Let me carry that for you," Xander said and reached for Tatiana's case.

"I'll be right back," Xander said.

"Okay," I nodded.

I hugged Leona, Tatum, and Jacory.

"I can't believe y'all put all of this together for me."

"It wasn't us. Xander called us last night, laid out the plan, and then delegated assignments," Leona chuckled.

"He wasn't playing with us either. He was calling and texting for updates," Tatum added.

"You got a great one, babe. He really cares about you and wanted this to happen for you. I'm jealous I didn't think of it first," Leona said.

"Well, I love y'all and so appreciate all of this. It was perfect."

"It was perfect. We are leaving. We will call you tomorrow, babe, okay?" Leona said after we hugged.

"Love you," Tatum said as we hugged.

"Love you, too."

"Xander, I will take this easel and picture back with me. Y'all can pick it up whenever you're ready," Jacory announced.

"Cool, good looking," Xander replied.

"We're not going home?" I asked Xander.

"No, we have other plans."

We waved goodbye to everyone.

"Where we are going is on the other side of the bluff. Come on," Xander said and took my hand.

"Thank you," I said as we walked hand in hand.

He looked down at me and smiled. "Of course."

We rounded the corner and, in a clearing, sat a vast rainbow-colored hot air balloon.

"Wow."

I'd never seen a hot air balloon in real life. It was massive. Two men greeted us and helped me into the enormous wicker basket attached to the balloon.

"I guess I should've asked if you were afraid of heights," Xander said.

"I'm not today."

The pilot went over the safety features and rules before he motioned to the man on the ground that he was ready to go.

The balloon slowly rose into the air. I watched as everything beneath us became smaller and further away. The balloon's smooth ride gave way to a feeling of weightlessness. While I was in the basket, I wasn't worried about going back into the kitchen, missing my Papa, sadness, or grief. Everything around us was quiet. We could only hear the sound of the air blowing into the balloon.

Xander held on to me as we admired the beauty of the bluffs and the river below us. We stayed on a northern path and made it to one of the two waterfalls in Sable Falls.

"Look how beautiful that is," I said.

The mighty rush of water from Kandake Falls gracefully and beautifully cascaded down the rocks into a plunge pool below. The frothy mist created from the water hitting the deep blue plunge pool produced the perfect double rainbow. We could see the entire arch of both magnificent rainbows.

"I've taken this trip a hundred times, and this is the first time I've ever seen a double rainbow," the pilot said as he took a couple of quick pictures with his phone.

I smiled. "That's Papa."

"Yep, it is," Xander agreed.

After the beautiful balloon ride, we walked hand in hand back to the truck.

"Are you tired?" Xander asked.

"Nope."

"Good because I have one more place that I want to take you."

"Let's go!"

We walked back to the truck and saw Chef Perry waiting with a cooler on his shoulder.

"It's all ready for you," Chef Perry said and passed the bag to Xander.

"I appreciate it," Xander said.

"It's my pleasure. Enjoy," Chef Perry replied.

We drove into an area of Sable Falls I'd never been to before.

"When was the last time you went to the drive-in?"

"Movies?" I asked.

"Yes," he chuckled. "The drive-in movie."

"I think my mother took me once when I was young. I probably was about seven or eight. I don't even remember what we saw."

"Well, I'm taking you to the drive-in," he said.

"There's a drive-in in Sable?"

"Yep, it's right there," he answered and pointed to the large neon sign ahead of us.

"Really? This is so exciting. What's showing?"

"You have the choice between Larenz Tate and Omar Epps. *Menace II Society* and *Love Jones* or *Love and Basketball* and *The Wood*," Xander said.

"That is an impossible choice! I want to see *Love Jones* and *Love and Basketball*. I know we can't switch so, I'm going with Omar," I decided.

"Good choice. I probably would've chosen Larenz for *Menace II Society*, but you picked the girly movies so that cool," Xander said.

"Girly! I like *Menace II Society* too, but how can I pass up Mike, Roland, and Slim reminiscing?"

"True, it's a solid choice," Xander said.

Xander paid for our tickets and then found a parking space in the center of the screen. There were tons of cars already there and parked. People were set up in chairs in front of their vehicles. Some cars backed in with their hatchbacks open, and people were set up in the back waiting for the movie to begin.

Xander got out the truck and retrieved the cooler he'd gotten from Chef Perry.

Chef Perry had packed everything from fried chicken sliders to cucumber and pickled blackberry salad.

"This all looks delicious," I said.

"Yeah, he outdid himself," Xander replied.

We ate the food while we watched the previews of upcoming movies. After we finished eating, Xander packed up the containers and put away the cooler.

"Let's sit in the back," Xander said.

He pulled out a blanket and laid it across both of us once I was nestled next to him in the back seat.

"*A*ngel," I felt Xander gently nudge me.

"Yes?" I sat up with a start and looked around.

"We fell asleep," he laughed.

The credits were rolling for the second movie.

"We are trash!" I replied, joining him in his laughter.

"I didn't see any of the second movie. The song playing with the credits woke me up."

"Well, so much for making out at the drive-in."

"Maybe next time."

"Definitely, next time," I continued to laugh.

*X*ander

The mood in the truck was completely opposite of what it was when Angel and I had started out this morning. Earlier she hadn't said much and looked so sad. After the drive-in, she kept smiling and looking at me between texting with her friends and laughing.

"You had a good day?" I asked after we pulled into the garage.

"Today was the best day ever. Thank you so much." Angel answered with a broad smile.

She never had to say thank you. Her smile was my reward.

"Anything for you, Angel."

We kissed before we went into the house.

*M*y family stayed for ten days before Dad had to pry my mother away from Man. She promised she would be back the following weekend to see him even though the drive was a solid two and a half hours. Tatiana went down to St. Helane with Mom to help her prepare for Man's christening.

"He is down," Angel announced when she returned to the living room. "He is going to be confused in the morning when his BGE is not here to hold him all day."

Mom heard Angel call her grandmother BG and decided she wanted it as her name instead of Granny or Grandma. Angel added the E to the moniker. Her name was BGE – best grandma ever.

My mother loved the name and she adored Angel. She had a whole pep talk with me about making sure I treated Angel right because I was lucky to have her. I agreed but thought it was funny that my mother told me I was fortunate to have someone. I thought it was usually the other way around.

Angel sat next to me on the couch. I pulled her close and wrapped my arm around her shoulder. As much as I enjoyed having my family with me, it hadn't left me much time to explore my lady. I would miss them but welcomed the time and opportunity to learn every single part of Angel.

"Yeah, it's only a matter of time before she's coming up here to drive him back down with her for weeks at a time. How do you feel about that?"

Angel sat up and looked at me.

"What?" I asked, confused by her reaction.

"I have a say?" she asked.

"Of course, you do. I want you to be comfortable with Man being gone. When Mom finally asks, because she is, I want us to agree."

"Alexander are you trying to make me fall in love with you?" she asked.

"Is it working?"

"I think it is."

"Good." I leaned over and kissed her.

"You know I would never disagree with your mother taking Man. She should be around him as much as she wants. I will just have to find something to do with myself while he's away."

"How about you work on developing new flavor profiles? I've watched you sketch a lot more in the past few days."

"When I tell you that I've been dreaming of new flavors all the time! I've never had so many ideas come to me at once," she said.

"That's a good thing, right?"

"I think so. I think it means I'm getting my mojo back, but at the same time, I'm not ready to be back in the restaurant environment. At this point, I think it has less to do with Papa and more to do with Man."

"Humph, do we need to find some help for him?"

"Hell no! I am the help! I wouldn't be able to go to a kitchen worried about someone taking care of him. Plus, you have a thing for nannies," she laughed.

"I do," I laughed.

"How about I order whatever you need to do whatever you want here in the kitchen. We have space to add the cold counter and a blast chiller. Would you like that?"

"I would," she replied, smiling, "Man and I can create away in there."

"Exactly. Mom wouldn't stop talking about how delicious the bonbons were. Thank you for making her a box to take home. I'm sure they won't make the entire drive," I laughed.

"I'm going to make her some more when we go down for the christening. I would also like to make some chocolate *Man* candy bars for the reception. That's one of the special molds I'm going to order. I want to do a couple flavors and have Maximus' name and birthday across the front of the chocolate," Angel said.

"That is so dope. Mom is going to be so excited."

"Yeah, that's one of the ideas that I jotted down. I've been thinking more and more about a chocolate bar. I would like to play around with chocolate-infused alcoholic drinks, desserts, and confections. Like I keep seeing live jazz acts in a small intimate area that smells of pure, rich chocolate," she gushed.

I could see it, too.

"We don't have anything like that here," I said.

"I know. I dreamt about it. Then I woke up and tried to remember everything I saw. It felt real when I was dreaming about it. Everyone I knew was there laughing and enjoying the chocolate and the music. You were there, too."

"I'm going to be wherever you are, so I'm not surprised. What would you name it; if you were to have something like that?" I asked.

She stood and walked to the kitchen and I followed.

"Midnight," she answered.

"Midnight...I love it," I responded.

"It's sexy, right? I would model it after the jazz clubs in Harlem during prohibition."

"That's a dope idea. When do you want to start working on it?" I asked.

"No time soon. It's just a thought right now. I was coming over here to clean the kitchen. You already did it?"

"Yeah, while you were putting Man down."

She put her arms around my neck. I backed her up until she rested against the island.

"Thank you," she said.

"For what?"

"Being you."

I leaned into her for a kiss. I adored the way her body melted into mine. I loved how soft her lips were. I pressed against her trying to get us closer, although it was impossible. I lifted her up and sat her on the kitchen island. We continued to kiss. I could smell her arousal and it was driving me crazy. I knew I said I wouldn't rush her, but I had to ask.

"Angelica."

"Yes?" she purred.

"Can I taste you?"

She looked into my eyes and said, "Please."

"Are you sure?"

"Positive," she responded.

"Here?"

"Wherever you want," she said.

My heart was beating out of my chest. I took a few deep breaths to calm myself down. I wanted this woman more than I could ever explain.

I lifted her legs and pulled her towards me. After quickly discarding her shorts and underwear, I leaned in to inhale her sweet, fresh scent, which left me feeling heady. Licking my lips, I admired how well-groomed she was. There wasn't even a landing strip, just the way I liked it.

"Angelica, you are perfect," I moaned.

Holding on to her hips to keep her in place, I placed several teaser kisses on and around her center.

"Mmmm," she moaned as she gripped the island.

She tasted as sweet as she smelled.

She continued to moan as I pleasured her. Spreading her legs further apart and rocking her hips into my face, she encouraged me to continue.

I enjoyed hearing her moans of pleasure. I loved the way she got wetter with each swipe of my tongue. I adored hearing her say my name when I inserted my finger into her tightness. By the way, she gripped my head and held it in place, I knew she was about to come.

"Alexander," she sang as her back arched off the counter.

I continued to kiss her until she calmed down.

"Angel, you're crying, are you okay? Did I hurt you?" I asked, pulling her into my arms. "I'm sorry, I shouldn't have rushed you. I mean, I didn't want to rush you into anything..."

"No, no, you didn't hurt me. You didn't rush me. I wanted this and it was amazing. I have no idea why I'm crying, but I can't stop," she said while wiping her tears.

"Are you sure..."

She nodded and continued to cry.

I didn't know what to do, so I held her until she calmed down.

After she stopped crying, she said, "I promise you didn't hurt me or do anything I didn't want to. I've fantasized about how it would feel when you touched me and this was so much better than I imagined. I just don't think I was ready for all those feelings to hit me like that. I feel so stupid."

"No, don't feel like that. Are you sure you're good?"

"Stop asking. I'm fine," Angel smiled.

"Now you know what this mouth do," I remarked with a wink.

"Shut up," she laughed.

*A*ngel

"You cried?" Leona whispered even though there was no reason to.

"Did he hurt you or something," Tatum whispered as well.

"No, it was amazing. The absolute best thing I've ever felt in my life; sheer pleasure, but for some reason, I cried. So that's not normal?"

I was visiting with the girls. I'd told them about my first cunnilingus experience and my weird reaction.

"It's not normal, but if that mouth is doing what it's supposed to do, maybe you will cry. Hell, it's been so long since someone had their mouth on me; I would probably cry too! I don't know what's going to happen once you finally get the dick," Tatum said.

"I'm ready," I announced.

"She's growing up right before our eyes," Tatum said and wiped a fake tear.

"I know, right?" Leona added.

"Okay, so look. If the dick is good and you cry, babe, just cry. Some of us will never experience it that good that we well up with emotion," Tatum said.

"Do you know when you want to do it?" Leona asked.

"Soon," I said definitively. "I've never wanted to have sex with anyone, but I almost feel like I can't control myself with Xander. Have you ever felt like that?"

"I have once and when I finally got it. My mind was blown. I've never had it that good since," Leona said.

Both Tatum and I looked at Leona.

"So, are you going to share?" I asked.

"No, it happened. It shouldn't have, and I've moved on," Leona shrugged.

"Ohhkay," Tatum started. "So, friend who doesn't keep secrets, let's go and get you on some birth control because I know you don't want another little Man running around after your first time. Do some research and talk to BG to see which option she thinks you should choose. Then let us know when you plan on getting it on so we can watch Man. You don't want this little baby interrupting the fun."

Tatum tickled Man, causing him to laugh.

"For sure. Also, talk to Xander about getting his STI testing done. You've waited all this time; you don't want to mess around and contract some crap you can't get rid of. I know you trust him, but it's better safe than sorry," Leona added.

"Okay...okay...I'm excited."

"You don't have to give us any details once it happens, but if that dick makes you cry too, you need to marry his ass," Tatum laughed.

"Immediately," Leona laughed.

⠿⠿⠿ ⠶⠶ ⠿⠿⠿ ⠶⠶ ⠿⠿⠿

"*H*ow is the baby doing?" BG asked.

"You saw the pictures I sent, right? He's growing more every day."

"Yes, I saw them. You sound happy," BG said.

"I am."

I'd called BG after I put Maximus down for a nap.

"Let me guess," BG said. "You and Xander finally told the truth about your feelings for each other?"

"Huh?" I laughed. I hadn't mentioned liking Xander to BG.

"Of course, that's what it is," BG surmised. "You told him or he told you?"

"BG, how did you know?"

"Girl, I have been teaching sex since I was your age. I can tell when two people are into each other, even if I'm not in their presence. You talk about him like he walks on water. He speaks of you like you saved his life."

"You've only spoken to him once, BG."

"That one conversation was enough. When a man is into a woman, he doesn't hide it, and Xander is definitely not hiding it. So, tell me about the conversation."

I told BG about the conversations Xander and I had about our relationship.

"You haven't had sex yet, huh?"

"BG..."

"What? It's just sex, Angelica. Are you planning on it?"

"Actually, that's why I wanted to talk to you. I need to get on some birth control."

"Oh, that's easy. I thought you wanted some tricks or tips," BG responded.

"I've sat through enough of your classes to know most of the stuff you've taught."

"Birth control is a good idea. Ask your GYN which one will allow for the maximum protection but be easily stopped when you are ready to have babies. I'm going to put you a care package together. I have a great lube that a black female-owned company just launched. It's a perfect consistency, not sticky or greasy. It mimics natural lubrication to a tee. They also have some soft, malleable toys that you both may like," BG said.

"The way I've been feeling, I don't think I will need any lube."

"You can never be too wet. That's a common misconception that women have. If sex lasts long enough, or the position changes, some natural moisture will dry up. That lube can be important. Dry sex is not fun for either party. Now with these toys, don't introduce anything into the bedroom until you've talked to him about it. Some men, mostly those who've never had a real sex education class, are not comfortable with toys. So, don't just spring anything on him."

"Yes, ma'am."

"He makes you happy, huh?"

"He enhances my happiness, yes."

"Now that's my Angelica. You create your own happiness. He can only enhance it. I'm happy you're happy," BG said.

"That's what you taught me. Oh, and I've been back in the kitchen."

"You have?"

"Yes, not in the restaurant, but I've made some chocolates, and I've been coming up with new flavors."

"You have?" BG repeated.

"Yeah, did I tell you about the double rainbow I saw on Papa's birthday?"

"No, but you remember Quincy loved rainbows," BG said.

"I know. After I saw it, I started dreaming about flavors and everything. I know it was his way of telling me to move forward," I said.

"I am so happy to hear that, Angelica," BG said.

"Oh, I want you to come here for Man's christening. Xander asked me to be Maximus' godmother."

"He did? That's a special honor," BG said.

"It is. I was surprised, but so excited."

"I bet you were. I wouldn't miss it," BG said.

Xander

"I didn't think you would still be awake," I said after leaning down to kiss Angel.

After walking in the house, I found her sitting on the living room couch, listening to music.

"You said you were going to be home late and I missed you," she said.

I loved coming home to Angel.

"I missed you, too. Let me take a quick shower. I'll be right back."

I knew I smelled just like the kitchen. I'd been helping because we'd hired some new staff. I wanted to make sure they stayed on task and knew their way around the kitchen.

"Okay," she replied.

I stopped in Man's room on the way to mine. He was sleeping with light music playing in the background.

After taking my shower and changing into my pajama pants and a wife-beater, I met Angel back in the front room.

She'd put out a charcuterie tray, a bottle of wine and two glasses.

"This looks good," I said, sitting down next to her.

"I found some prosciutto, but then I came across jamón ibérico, which you know is ham cured to perfection. I had to put both on a tray with fresh Parmigiano Reggiano and some blueberries."

"You found this jamón ibérico in the market?" I asked.

"Yep."

"I need to get to the market more often."

I took a slice of the ham and popped it into my mouth along with the cheese and fruit.

"The cured ham is terrific with the bitterness of the cheese and sweetness of the blueberries."

I took a sip of my wine.

"I know, I've been snacking on it all day," Angel smiled.

"How was your day?" I asked.

"It was good. I had an appointment today and got this implanted."

She lifted her arm to show me a small bandage on her upper arm.

"What is it?"

"Birth control. I'm ready," she said.

"Right now?" I asked, grinning.

She laughed, "I mean, not right now, but I don't want to wait too much longer."

"You're not saying this because of what happened on the kitchen count..."

"No!" she interrupted. "Well, yes...but no."

"Which one is it?"

"No, I'm not saying this because I feel rushed, because I don't. Hell yeah, because of what happened in the kitchen. I'm trying to see how it all comes together. I mean if that was like that then..." She shrugged as her words trailed off.

I laughed and shook my head.

"You are silly. For real, though. Is this what you want? I mean us." I pointed between us.

"Absolutely," she said. "So, I need for you to get your STI testing done. I did mine today."

"I have a physical for work at the end of the week. I will request all the tests."

"Then I will be ready after that," she said.

"Alright, let me plan something and make it special for you. Can I do that?"

"Yes, I would like that," Angel said.

⁑⁂⁑ ⁂⁑ ⁂⁑⁂

J moved my physical appointment up by two days. If Angel was ready, then I was too! I had all the STI testing done, and within two days, I received my clean bill of health. Angel received all negative test results as well.

I'd rented a penthouse suite at the hotel in the center of downtown for the weekend. I took a couple of days off, so Angel and I could take our time. I wanted it to be unique and memorable. I also wanted to give her space and opportunity to change her mind.

Angel and Man went over to her friends' house earlier in the day while I was still finalizing plans. Man would stay with Leona and Tatum.

Angel would change at their house, then I would send a car to pick her up and take her to the hotel.

Having connections in the culinary world worked out when planning romantic dinners away from the crowd. The head chef at the hotel prepared dinner and it would be served to us on the rooftop overlooking the city.

I was both nervous and excited. Nervous because I wanted everything to be perfect for Angel and excited because I was about to make love to the woman of my dreams.

The 360-degree views of the city in the penthouse were breathtaking. The hotel staff did a great job of preparing the room for our stay. The king-sized bed was sprinkled with red and white rose petals. There were little candles lit everywhere, which I thought was against some fire code. I touched one and realized they were all fake.

While the culinary staff was out on the rooftop setting up the table, I showered and changed into my black suit and white shirt. I left the first couple buttons on my shirt open and put a houndstooth handkerchief in my jacket pocket. My black loafers finished the look.

Car Service: I have picked up Ms. Saint Rose and we are on our way to you. ETA is 15 mins.

The nervousness really kicked in after reading that text message. I turned on the speakers filling the room with smooth jazz. Then poured myself a shot of añejo tequila to calm my nerves.

Fifteen minutes later, the doorbell rang. I took a deep breath and opened the door.

Angel took my breath away. Her hair was out of the braids. She wore it big and full like an afro. She had on a short, white dress that hugged her curves the exact way I'd planned on hugging them later.

"Welcome," I smiled and stepped to the side, giving her space to enter.

She sexily sauntered past me in a pair of white stilettos that made her legs look longer. Her signature fresh smell followed her into the room.

"Xander, this is beautiful," Angel said, looking around the room.

"No, you are beautiful, Angelica. White was made to be worn by you." I took her hand and encouraged her to do a quick spin.

"I wore it for you," she said and put her arm around my neck.

"Excellent choice," I replied.

I gave her a quick kiss.

"Come, let's have some wine while we wait for them to finish setting up for dinner."

I poured us both a glass of wine while Angel stood looking at the spectacular view of the city.

"What are you thinking about?" I asked while passing her a glass of wine.

I wrapped my arms around her. She rested her back against my chest.

"I was just thinking about how beautiful this view is. And how lucky I am."

"Lucky?"

"Yep, to be alive, Black and talented and happy. It's a fierce combination," Angel said.

"You're happy?"

"The happiest I've been in a very long time," she smiled.

"Dinner is served," one of the culinary staff announced.

Stepping out onto the rooftop, we were met with soft jazz music filling the perfect summer evening air. The lights of the tall buildings added to the beautiful backdrop that was downtown Sable Falls.

White lights were strung from posts around the rooftop's perimeter, adding additional illumination to the beautifully organized table for two in the center of the floor. The white tablecloth covered table for two was set with gold and white place settings and a vase of white roses in the center of the table.

"Xander," Angel said as she took in all the décor. "This is beautiful."

"Not nearly as beautiful as you," I responded while pulling out her chair.

We feasted on a three-course meal prepared by one of the best chefs in Sable Falls. After we finished our food, the culinary staff presented us both with a small covered dish.

"What is this?" Angel asked.

"Dessert."

The servers simultaneously removed the lids.

The plates contained three perfectly plated chocolate confections: one bonbon, one truffle, and one solid chocolate square.

She looked at the chocolate closely.

"These look...oh my gawd, they are Patrico's chocolates! Where did these come from?"

"I sent for them."

She immediately popped one of the truffles in her mouth.

"Ohhh," she leaned her head to the side and closed her eyes. "Did you try one?"

"No," I replied.

She reached onto my plate and picked up the truffle.

"Here, open," she directed.

She placed the chocolate in my mouth.

"Wow, these are delicious."

"I can't believe you did this for me, thank you."

"I have one more thing for you."

I slid the small gift box across the table.

She picked up the box and shook it.

"Is it more candy?"

"Sorta, open it and see," I instructed.

Angel opened the box.

"Xander, are these chocolate diamonds?"

"Yeah, I never see you wear big earrings, so I figured you would like a pair of diamond earrings."

"And chocolate because..." she started.

"Because you love chocolate and they are unique just like you," I finished.

"I've never owned diamonds before."

"I've never purchased diamonds for anyone, so it's a first for both of us."

She quickly took her earrings out of her ears and replaced them with the chocolate diamonds.

Her bright smile made me smile.

"Thank you," she said with a smile.

"Will you dance with me?"

"Yes," she replied, her smile stretching more broadly across her face.

We danced to the music while holding each other close.

"You know if you want to change your mind, you can, right?"

"Why would I want to do that?" she asked, pulling back to look at me.

I shrugged lightly. "Just making sure."

"I think about you when I touch myself. Why would I keep doing that when I can feel the real thing?"

If I thought she could take it, I would've bent her over the balcony and had her right there. I knew I had to take my time, so instead, I took her hand and led her back into the penthouse.

"Xander," Angel said when she saw the bedroom with all the roses and candles. "This is so beautiful."

"Not as beautiful as you, Angelica."

I gently wrapped my hand around her neck, leaned down, and kissed her. I applied a little pressure, and she moaned, letting me know it was okay. I sprinkled kisses along her jawline down to her collarbone to her ear and back to her mouth.

I reached behind her and found the zipper on her dress and released it. Looking into her eyes, I waited until the dress hit the ground before I stepped back to take her all in. She wore a white lace bra and panty set that looked amazing against her skin, but I couldn't wait to get all of it off her.

I kissed her again, lightly, then used my forefinger to gently follow her body's contours between her breasts, over her navel, and across the thin fabric of her panties.

"Is this where you touch yourself when you think of me?"

"Yes," she moaned as I continued to run my finger across her panties. Feeling how soaked her panties were had me so hard, but I had to take my time.

"Show me how you touch yourself." I pulled back and nodded towards the bed.

She walked over to the bed, laid down, and spread her legs. I started unbuttoning my shirt and kicked off my shoes while watching her unsnap her bra, giving me a full view of magnificent perfection. She grabbed one of her hardened nipples between her thumb and forefinger and rolled it while her other hand slid into her panties.

"Ohh," she moaned.

That moan almost sent me over. I had to breathe through it. She was so sexy and I wanted her so bad.

I quickly removed my pants and underwear, kicking them to the side.

Stroking myself slowly, I watched Angel pleasure herself.

She pulled her bottom lip between her teeth as she watched me stroke myself.

"Xander, you are beautiful," she said. "Can I taste you?"

After climbing on the bed, I situated myself at her lips. She opened her mouth wide, ready to receive me.

"Damn," I hissed.

The warmth of her mouth combined with the wetness was sensory overload. I didn't think we would make it this far tonight, but I wasn't complaining. She positioned herself to take as much of me in as she could. She attempted a little more and gagged.

"You okay?" I asked.

She nodded without removing her mouth. She used her hand to guide me in and out using a suction that I'd never felt before. She didn't need any instructions like, watch your teeth or be gentle with my nuts. She sucked and touched everything just the way I liked it. I moved in and out of her mouth while replacing her hand in her panties with mine.

She was soaking wet. The room was filled with the sounds of her sucking and my fingers penetrating her moisture.

I felt myself getting close just as she arched her back off the bed.

"Xander," she said and held my hand in place while she rocked against it. She rocked until she stiffened and her body collapsed.

I almost came watching her.

"I need you inside me," she moaned.

I climbed on top of her and kissed her. She reached between us and stroked me. Her hand felt almost as good as her mouth.

I lined myself up with her opening.

"I want you so bad," I said.

"Take me," she moaned.

I grabbed the lube, and after using a generous amount, I slowly pushed my way into her tight, wet pussy. After feeling a little resistance, I paused and kissed her again.

"You are so beautiful," I whispered into her ear.

I felt her relax a little, so I pushed some more.

"You feel amazing, Angelica," I said.

She relaxed a little more, so I pushed more.

I felt her grip tighten on my back.

"Are you good?"

"Yes," she said.

"Do you want me to stop?"

"No," she whispered. "Please don't stop."

Starting with short strokes, I slowly worked my way all the way in. I paused again to make sure she was okay. I saw a tear fall from her eye.

"I'm okay," she assured me.

I continued to stroke her until I felt her moving her hips with mine. When her thrust became more intense, I knew it was on.

I propped myself on my hands so I could watch my hardness, drenched in her wetness, moving in and out until I felt her walls tighten around me.

"Xander, I'm coming," she announced.

She locked her legs around my back and rode her wave of ecstasy. I tried to hold on, but I came right behind her.

I collapsed beside her and pulled her close.

"Are you okay?" I said while still trying to catch my breath.

"I'm better than okay. That was amazing. Let's do it again."

"Okay," I laughed. "I need a few minutes."

*A*ngel

 I kept humming "Tonight is the Night" in my head while Xander and I soaked in the large tub.

Resting with my back on his chest, I enjoyed the lavender-scented bubble bath. He told me he put a bath bomb and Epson salt in the water. Despite my enthusiasm to go another round, I was sore.

I enjoyed every second of sex with Xander, even the painful parts because they didn't last long. He was patient and gentle. He watched me and took his cues from my reactions and not my words. I appreciated him. I'd watched so many movies and heard about women saying their first time was painful, uneventful, and disappointing. I couldn't relate to any of that. Well...it did hurt but not the entire time. The second time was not nearly as painful as the first.

Xander's planning of the evening was way more than I'd expected or hoped for. He didn't miss one detail; from the chauffeured ride to the hotel to the penthouse to the rose petals on the bed, I was in awe.

"Are you feeling okay?" Xander asked while squeezing water from the towel against my arm.

"I'm a little sore, but I'm good."

"We probably should give you a few days to heal," he said.

"Yeah, but I really enjoyed it. I love this penthouse and this evening was perfect."

Maxwell's Essentials playlist serenaded us as we quietly soaked in the tub.

"I have a question. Why did you help me on the plane?" Xander said.

"Ummm...I noticed you when we were at the gate. I kept waiting to see a woman come and sit down next to you. I wondered if she would be tall and statuesque or short and feisty. I guessed she would be someone where in between. The way you gently handled Man made me envious of the woman who was afforded that same touch. Then I caught myself because I'd never fantasized about a man's touch, let alone a man who I didn't know and was obviously in a relationship. When she never showed up and we got on the plane, I almost felt like it was my responsibility to help. I felt so drawn to you and Maximus. I couldn't explain it."

"I looked for you at baggage claim," Xander said.

"I walked so fast to the baggage claim, almost pushing people out of the way to get my bag. I couldn't stay and come face to face with the woman who was with the man and baby who had stolen my heart in a matter of minutes. I got my bag and almost ran out of that airport."

"I thought about you every day after that," I admitted.

"I thought about you every day after that, too," Angel said.

"I love you, Angel."

Looking into his eyes after quickly turning around, I saw all the sincerity I'd hoped to see when those words were said.

"I thought about telling you during dinner. I thought about it while we were making love, but I didn't want it to sound cliché – because it's true. I don't know when I knew, but I've known for a while."

145

"I love you, Xander."

I climbed on his lap and kissed him.

"Slow down. We need to wait," Xander cautioned.

"We can't do anything?" I lifted one eyebrow.

"I mean – we can try some other things," he said.

11

Angel

*M*rs. Northcott, who'd told me to call her Momma Pearl, had finalized all the planning for Man's christening. I'd purchased BG a ticket to fly in for the ceremony. I had also been helping with the menu for the family gathering afterward.

I told Momma Pearl about the chocolate bars I was going to create. She was so excited about them. I smiled when she said all the women at the church would be jealous when she told them that her son's girlfriend was a famous chocolatier.

Xander and I had settled on a cute christening outfit for Maximus that we found at the baby boutique in the mall. After my first visit there, when Man and I had our mall debacle, I'd gone back often and had become friendly with the store owner.

"Pieta has the room all prepared for your BG," Xander announced.

I jumped when he spoke. I was so deep in thought; I didn't hear him come in.

"I didn't mean to scare you," he chuckled.

"I'm just trying to make sure I have everything packed for Man and me. I mean, I know there are stores there in case I forget something, but I'm trying not to."

He walked into the room and roped his arms around my waist, pulling me close. He lightly kissed my lips and then my neck.

"Packing is what has you concerned?" Xander asked.

"No, it's not packing; it's BG. I don't know if she will see how happy I really am or if she will spend this time trying to convince me that I need to be back in the kitchen. I can stop those conversations on the phone, but I can't stop them in person."

"Are you happy?"

"I am," I answered.

"She loves you; she will see it. If she doesn't see it, then she doesn't want to. Then that's on her."

"You're right."

"I need you to be happy and enjoy this long weekend. It's Man's christening, and it's the first time our families will meet. I'm not going to let anyone, or anything, spoil this for us, okay?"

"Okay," I replied with a smile.

"This smile," Xander pointed, "is my goal this whole weekend."

"I love you," I said as I kissed him.

"I love you, too."

Xander

We rented a Sprinter to drive down to St. Helane. Jacory, Leona, and Tatum rode down with us. Everett, Kerry, and their kids followed behind us. I'd arranged for a driver to pick up Angel's grandmother from the airport in St. Helane. She would meet us at the rental Leona had found. After the christening, BG would stay a few more days with us in Sable Falls.

The rental house was an estate. It had enough bedrooms and bathrooms for all of us, including Everett and his family, to stay comfortably.

"Oh, you showed out with this rental," Tatum said.

"I know. It's a corporate house. They use it for meetings and whatnot. I asked the staff to put everyone's names on their doors. I figured Kerry and her family would want the guest house in the back. The rooms are all together, so you won't be away from the kids. The Northcott-Saint Rose group will be on the right side of the house with BG, and the singles will be on the left side. We have dinner being catered tonight with a movie outside. I will give you the rest of the itinerary tonight," Leona said.

We all went our separate ways and found our rooms.

We chose one of the three rooms in that wing of the house to sleep in. I went back out to get the rest of our things from the Sprinter when I saw a black sedan pull up to the house's front. I was almost positive it was Mrs. Saint Rose.

I abandoned our things in the Sprinter to go and welcome her. The driver got out of the car and walked around to open the rear passenger door. When Angel described her BG, I was thinking of a standard grandmother like my grandmother: older, maybe a little heavier, gray hair tightly curled or somewhat scarce. I was not prepared to see a black patent leather stiletto hit the ground, followed by another. Then a tall, almost six-foot, wrinkle-free, bronze-skinned woman with long salt and pepper locs stepped out of the car. She had on a sleeveless dress that showed off some major guns. BG was gorgeous. I could definitely see where Angel got it from. She wore large black sunglasses, but I could tell when she made eye contact and recognized me.

"Mrs. Saint Rose?"

"Xander," she said with a smile as she removed her glasses.

"Yes, ma'am," I replied with a grin.

"It's a pleasure to finally meet you."

"The pleasure is mine. I will grab your bags and show you where we are in the house."

"Thank you," she smiled.

I took her suitcase from the driver, gave him a tip. Then showed Mrs. Saint Rose into the house.

Rounding the corner, I could hear Angel and Man laughing. She was obviously doing something silly enough to make him laugh out loud.

"Hey, look who I found," I said and stepped to the side.

"BG!" Angel said and quickly made her way into her grandmother's arms.

"Hi, beautiful!" Mrs. Saint Rose responded.

I took Man from Angel so they could fully enjoy the moment.

"I've missed you!" Mrs. Saint Rose said.

"I missed you, too!" Angel replied, wiping tears.

"I've met Xander, but I haven't had the pleasure of meeting this young man in person," Mrs. Saint Rose said.

"This is Maximus. Maximus, this is my BG not to be confused with your BGE," Angel said.

Mrs. Saint Rose reached for Maximus. He flung himself forward into her arms and immediately went for the chunky necklace she was wearing.

"Oh, look at him, all this hair and these cheeks! He is so beautiful!" Mrs. Saint Rose said.

"Thank you," I responded.

"BG, your room is over here," Angel said.

I followed them to her room, carrying BG's suitcases.

"I will try to pry him away from you now. I'm sure you want to catch up," I said and reached for Man.

"We will get more acquainted later, Mr. Maximus," Mrs. Saint Rose said. "You too, Xander."

"Yes, ma'am," I replied with a smile as Maximus and I left the room.

⠿⠿⠿⠿ ⠁⠈⠁ ⠿⠿⠿⠿ ⠁⠈⠁ ⠿⠿⠿⠿

J went to the other side of the house to check out the rooms.

"It's nice over here, too," I said to Jacory.

"Lee outdid herself. What are you and Man doing over here? Where is Angel?"

"Mrs. Saint Rose just arrived. I wanted to give them some alone time."

"This is your first time seeing BG?" Jacory asked.

"I'd seen pictures of her, but I thought they were old pictures. I had no idea who she was when she pulled up."

"I was at Mr. Saint Rose's funeral. I saw at least four men trying to help her out and a couple more waiting in the wings. Niggas was at the house immediately, cutting grass, washing cars, taking out trash and shit. It was something to see," Jacory chuckled.

"Was he a lot older than her?"

"I think he was a little older, but the years have just been great to her," Jacory finished.

"They have."

*A*ngel
    Leona and Tatum rushed over to see BG as soon as they heard she'd arrived. All three of us sat in her room, laughing and talking until the girls had to leave to prepare for the evening.

"Xander is more handsome in person," BG said after she and I were alone.

"Yeah, he is. He's also sweet and patient. Sometimes he reminds me of Papa."

"Does he?"

"Yeah, his calm demeanor and the way he handles business. His passion for his family and the people he cares about."

"Those are good traits," BG said.

"I think so. BG…"

"Yes?"

"I want us to have a good trip, and I want you to have a good time while you're here, so can we just go ahead and talk about the kitchen thing and get it off the table?" I rushed out.

She sat down the bed and patted the space next to her.

I sat down.

"You were concerned about me coming here and trying to force you to do something you've already told me you don't want to do?" BG said.

I exhaled, "Yes."

"Well, I'm not. I hadn't seen you this happy since before you went to culinary school. After that, you were so focused on chocolate and creating the next big thing."

"I felt like I had a lot to prove," I admitted.

"Yeah, I went with it because that's how your Papa was in the kitchen. Then he passed, and I didn't recognize you at all. I felt like I lost both you and Quincy at the same time. His death broke you, but now I see you and I realize that Quincy's death didn't break you. It was just the final straw.

You weren't happy before he died. His death just made all of that abundantly clear," BG explained.

"I wasn't happy or fulfilled, but I really didn't realize it either. I love chocolate, and I love food, but now I know I love it because I do, not because Papa did."

"You are full of joy, and it's written all over your face. I love it! So, no, I'm not here to convince you to do anything. I just want you to be happy."

I quickly wrapped my arms around her and we both cried.

"So, how's the sex?" BG asked after we stopped crying.

We both laughed.

"Amazing! It's better than I thought it could be."

"Good. I brought a few things for you," BG started before aiming a wink my way.

⁂

"There's my baby," Momma Pearl said as soon as she entered the house, making a beeline for Maximus.

I passed Maximus to Momma Pearl.

"Momma Pearl, this is my BG, Jean-Ann Saint Rose. BG, this is Xander's mother."

They hugged like they were old friends.

"It's a pleasure to meet you," BG said.

"The pleasure is mine," Momma Pearl said. "Angel looks just like you."

"I wish I could claim that beauty. She looks like her mother," BG said with a smile.

We all sat down to a beautifully decorated table.

"Everyone, this is Chef Herbert. An award-winning chef here in St. Helane. He prepared dinner for us tonight," Leona said.

"Thank you for allowing me to cook for you tonight. My partner and I have prepared an appetizer of firecracker prawns, our take on Asian flavors. It has some heat to it but not much. To cool your palate, we have a chilled cherry soup with fennel and sour cream. The entrée is a garlic herb stuffed chicken breast with mashed potatoes and green beans. For dessert, we have a green tea tiramisu in individual cups. Enjoy," Chef Herbert said.

"Jean-Ann, what do you for a living?" Momma Pearl asked.

"I'm a clinical sexologist," BG answered.

All my friends knew BG's profession, but Xander's people did not.

"Really?" Tatiana leaned in. "What exactly do you do?"

"Tati!" Momma Pearl scolded.

"No," BG laughed. "It's a common misconception for people to confuse what I do, which is totally hands-off, with what a sex surrogate does, which is more hands-on. I'm a licensed psychologist that focuses on sexual issues with couples and individuals. I pride myself in helping people learn how to pleasure themselves and their partners. I also teach 'how-to' classes, but again that's using props, strictly hands-off," BG explained.

"How to what?" Tatiana asked.

"Everything and probably some things you've never heard of," BG answered.

"We might need a class while you're here, Mrs. Saint Rose," Tatum said.

"We can," BG answered.

"Are your classes usually for men, women, single, married?" Momma Pearl asked.

"Anyone can attend depending on what you want to learn. I encourage people in all stages of relationships to attend," BG explained.

"What about the old adage about old dogs – new tricks?" Momma Pearl asked.

"I've seen couples well into their golden years revive their sex life after my classes," BG said.

"Oh yeah?" Momma Pearl said.

"Momma, you coming to the class?" Tatiana leaned in and looked down the table towards Momma Pearl.

"I'll be front row, center," Momma Pearl announced.

The whole table erupted in laughter.

"*I* think I put everything in here that he will need for the next couple days," I said while handing the diaper bag to Mr. Northcott.

Momma Pearl and Pop Northcott were taking Maximus back home with them until the christening ceremony.

"If it's not in there, we will get it, but I'm sure it's fine," Momma Pearl said.

"Okay, I will see you later, Maximus. Angel loves you," I said and kissed Man.

After leaning in and kissing him too, Xander closed the door and watched his parents drive away.

"Are you okay?" Xander asked.

"I think I'm good. I will let you know in the morning when Man is not there to give me my good morning kiss."

"I can take care of that for him," Xander said.

We laughed, laced fingers, and walked back into the rental house.

BG met us in the kitchen.

"Xander, can we have coffee together tomorrow morning?" BG asked.

"Yes, ma'am. I will take you to the best coffee spot in town," Xander answered.

"Great. Well, I'm going to my room. Good night," BG said.

"Good night," we both responded.

"Thank you for agreeing to spend some time with BG. It means a lot to me," I said once Xander and I were in our room.

"You love her, so I love her too," Xander said.

I wrapped my arms around his waist, got up on my tiptoes, and kissed him.

"I'm feeling better," I replied, smiling.

After my first time having sex, Xander had suggested that we wait to make sure I wasn't in any pain. Then I started my period, which was longer than usual because of the new birth control. We hadn't had the opportunity to have sex again, but I felt much better.

"Really?" Xander said and ran his thumb across my bottom lip.

I sucked his thumb into my mouth.

He quickly lifted me onto his waist and carried me to the bed.

The throb in my pussy and the fluttering in my stomach was over-whelming. I'd never been so attracted to a man. I longed for him to touch me.

Xander gently laid me on the bed and got on top of me.

"Tell me what you want," Xander said.

"I want to feel your lips on every part of my body. Then I want to feel you in my stomach like I did the last time. Make me come, more than once."

"Anything else," Xander asked while slowly moving down my body.

"No, but I reserve the right to add on if necessary."

"You can always have whatever you want," Xander said.

I sat up so he could pull my dress over my head. After discarding it on the floor, he made quick work of my bra and panties.

"Your body is amazing, Angelica."

He kissed his way down from my forehead, to my nose, then to my lips. I could feel the difference in the way Xander hungrily kissed me compared to the first time we were together. His gentle touch was replaced with authority and ferocity that turned me on even more. Kissing, licking, and sucking his way from my lips, around my collarbone and to my breasts. He was doing exactly as I requested. Pausing to suck one of my breasts into his mouth while massaging the other, he continued—past my stomach to my thighs. I spread my legs, ready to feel his tongue on my center.

"Slow down, Angelica. We have all night," he said as he feathered kisses on both my thighs.

The slow pace was sensual torture.

"You want me to kiss you here?" Xander asked and softly ran his finger over my center.

"Yes," I hummed.

"Like this?" he said and flattened his tongue against the hood of my clit.

"Exactly, like that," I answered while holding his head in place.

The vacuum-like suction from his mouth on my center almost took me over. He inserted one finger and continued to lick.

I felt my ascension forming in the pit of my stomach. Knowing it was going to be a strong one, I held on to his head and rode his face until my body seized.

"Xander," I called out as I rode the massive wave of ecstasy.

"That's my girl," Xander said after I calmed down.

Lining himself up with my opening, he asked, "You ready?"

"Hell yeah."

He spit on his massive member and forcefully slid it inside.

I locked my feet around his back and held him as he stroked me deeply. Each stroke hitting pleasure points I never knew existed.

"Wait," I said, pushing against him so he could slide out of me.

I turned over and got onto my hands and knees.

"You want it like this?" he asked.

"Yes, please."

The sensation of being entered from the back was different, but it felt so good. Xander held on to my hips and stroked me deeply.

"You feel amazing, Angelica," Xander moaned.

"It's all yours, Xander. I want to feel every inch," I moaned.

His grip on my hips tightened. His strokes went deeper, causing me to yell out some gibberish right before I climaxed.

"Damn, Angelica!" Xander called out as he climaxed.

Xander

"This is Pete's Diner. It's one of the oldest diners in St. Helane, and it was my first job," I said as I opened the door for Mrs. Saint Rose.

I led her to a booth near the window then sat down across from her.

"What can I getcha?" the waitress asked.

"I will have the French toast and a cup of coffee, please," Mrs. Saint Rose said.

"I will have the same, thank you," I answered.

"So, you grew up here?" Mrs. Saint Rose asked.

"Yes, ma'am. My childhood home is not too far from here."

"How did you end up in Sable Falls?"

"The culinary opportunities were better, so after I graduated from culinary school, I took a position at one of the restaurants there," I explained.

The waitress returned with our coffee.

"Do you have any future plans? My precious Angel is quite smitten with you. You met her during an extremely fragile time in her life. I just want to make sure you aren't wasting her time. I also want to make sure that you aren't just looking for a mother for Maximus. She needs to be taken care of and treated like the rare find that she is," Mrs. Saint Rose said then sipped her coffee.

"I appreciate you not mincing words and getting to the point. I have plans, all of which involve Angel. Not as my nanny, but as my wife and Maximus' mother. He will know that someone else birthed him into this world, but as soon as he got here, Angel picked him up and hasn't put him down. I want to marry her and build a life with her."

"I remember when Quincy told my father that he wanted to marry me. I wasn't there for the conversation, but Quincy told me that my father asked what can you bring to the table that she can't bring herself? So, I pose the same question to you. Angel is a culinary savant. There isn't anything that she can't perfect in the kitchen. She chose chocolate, but she could've done anything. People know her name and her confections around the world. Hell, there were three or four restaurants in Sable Falls that were fighting over her. What can you offer?"

Just then the waitress walked up and placed our French toast in front of us.

"Can I get you two anything else?" she asked.

"I'm good," I responded.

"No, nothing else, thank you," Mrs. Saint Rose answered.

"Nothing. Angel is a better chef than me, a better caregiver than me, and a better person than me. I know that she increases my value. I'm well aware that I would have the baddest chick in the culinary game wearing my ring. I know that she can decide to go back to London or anywhere else in the culinary world at any given moment and they would welcome her with open arms. She can do anything she puts her mind to, yet she chooses to put her mind to loving me and loving Man. I don't know how I got so lucky, but I am. I love her with a ferocity that scares me sometimes, but I know it still doesn't match her love. So, to the table? I can't bring anything to match her, but I can bring support. I will stand by her side and support whatever decisions that make her happy. I will stand in front of her if someone or something tries to come at her sideways. I will move heaven and earth to see her dreams come to pass," I finished.

Mrs. Saint Rose cut into her French toast and ate a piece.

Nodding, she said, "This is good."

"It is. They have some of the best French toast around," I agreed.

"Why should I believe what you say? People say a lot of words to get what they want," Mrs. Saint Rose said.

"I don't think you should believe what I say. You should watch what I do. Actions speak louder than words," I responded.

"Humph," she chuckled. "Quincy would've liked you."

"Angel has told me so much about him. I know I would've liked him, too."

"I will watch you, Alexander. Treat my Angel with care and treat her fairly. I know relationships have their ups and downs. That's to be expected. However, if you don't treat her with care and respect? I. Will. Fuck. You. Up. That's on all my dead relatives. I will burn this town to the ground over mine. You feel me?" she replied with a smile.

"Yes, ma'am. I feel you."

"Good. This coffee and French toast are delicious. Thank you for bringing me here," she said.

We finished our toast and coffee and enjoyed a non-life-threatening conversation. Mrs. Saint Rose went to the restroom while I paid for the check.

Angel: You still alive?

I quickly typed my response before Mrs. Saint Rose returned.

Xander: Barely – No lol

*A*ngel
    I chuckled and tucked my phone in my pocket.

"What's funny?" Tatum asked.

"BG obviously showed her Compton side to Xander."

"He ain't know BG was about that life, huh?" Tatum laughed.

"No," I laughed.

Leona, Tatum, Kerry, Tatiana, and I had just pulled up to the mall to find something to wear to the christening. Momma Pearl requested that we all wear blue and white.

I was hoping to find a simple dress and a pair of shoes. I had an alternate outfit that I packed, but I wasn't sold on it. I was hoping to find something better.

"I was thinking that after we finish shopping, we could get some seafood and have a seafood boil this evening and maybe play some games?" Leona said.

"That sounds fun. The kids are staying with my in-laws so we can play some adult games. Maybe BG will give us some tips," Kerry said.

"BG is always up for teaching a class or giving some tips," I laughed.

We shopped at several stores before I found a pretty light blue, double breasted blazer dress and a pair of cobalt blue pumps. We ordered coffee drinks from one of the kiosks and sat down to enjoy our beverages.

"Oh my gawd. Look at this silly girl," Kerry said.

She turned her phone and showed a video of Emmaline kissing on some poor man who didn't seem as thrilled as she was to be there.

"Who is that?" Tatum asked.

"That's Emmaline."

"The ex?" Tatum said.

"Yes, I thought I unfollowed her, but apparently she has two accounts. She is one of those people who will put stuff on social media to give the appearance that she is doing so much and doing so well. She put on a whole production when Xander broke up with her," Kerry said.

"I couldn't stand that bitch," Tatiana rolled her eyes.

"She said something about them breaking up on social media? Xander didn't mention it."

"That's because he probably didn't see it. You know my brother lives in a semi bubble. Once he was done with her, I'm sure he stopped following her," Tatiana said.

"I don't think he ever started back following her once they got back together," Kerry said. "If I recall correctly, that was one of their arguments. He didn't want to be all over social media and she did."

"I, for one, am so glad that bitch is gone. My brother is a planner and a dreamer. At every turn, she was shooting down his plans and encouraging him to make stupid moves," Tatiana said.

"She was toxic. I told Xander that when he first brought her around.

Everett just flat out hated her. He barely spoke to her. The little interaction he had with her was because of Xander. Then one day, Everett came home talking about look at Xander's nanny. I knew without anyone ever confirming it that he liked you and Emmaline's days were numbered," Kerry said.

"I didn't do anything to sabotage their relationship."

"Oh, girl, I know. Xander isn't that guy anyway. When he's with you, he's faithful. He really is one of the best men I know. I'm just happy you guys found each other. He's never smiled so much," Kerry said.

"After he met you on the plane, he mentioned you every day we talked until he found you. It wasn't a mistake that y'all found each other. I prayed for you. God is my best friend, so He be listening to me," Tatiana chuckled.

"I said the same thing when I saw Xander the first time. Didn't I, Lee?" Tatum said.

"Yes, she did," Leona confirmed.

"It was just something about their energy. I don't believe in soulmates, but if I did, I would say you two were made for each other," Tatum smiled.

"Y'all gon' make me cry."

"Well, we know someone who did make you cry," Tatum mumbled.

"Who made you cry?" Tatiana said.

"Oh my gawd," I said and covered my face.

"Your brother...but..." Tatum nodded but didn't finish.

"Cried like how? He did something to hurt you?" Tatiana asked.

"Nope, the complete opposite," Tatum said.

"Wait he's my brother...okay, no details but like...what?" Tatiana said.

"Like she know what that mou..." Tatum started.

"Tatum!" I tried to stop her.

"And you cried?" Kerry whispered the same way Leona did when I told them.

"Damn..." Tatiana said and sat back in her chair.

"I know, right?" Kerry leaned back also.

"Like your eyes misted or you..." Tatiana started.

"Like full out I need tissue cried," Tatum answered.

I nodded my head.

"I was speechless when she told us, too," Leona said.

"Call BG and tell her we all need a session, to-night!" Tatiana laughed.

Xander

It had been years since I'd been to my childhood church. They'd expanded the sanctuary and added comfortable, cushioned seats. When I was growing up, we had hard wooden pews that would give you splinters if you weren't careful. The service hadn't began yet, so people were standing around talking while music played softly in the background.

We all filed in and settled in the seats that Mom had reserved close to the front for us. Angel went straight for Man when she saw my mother standing and holding him. She'd been a trooper the last couple days, but I could tell she missed Man a lot.

"You look handsome in your all-white, Man," Angel smiled and kissed him.

"He's been great company," Mom said. "Thank you for letting him hang with his grandparents."

"Grandparents are the best," Angel smiled.

We left Man with Mom and sat down with our group.

"So, this is where you grew up, huh?" Angel asked.

"Yep, spent a ton of time here between church, bible school, and choir rehearsal."

"Choir rehearsal?" Angel lifted one eyebrow.

"I was forced. I hated singing. As soon as I was old enough to get a job, I volunteered to work on choir rehearsal night. If you missed choir rehearsal, then you couldn't sing," I shrugged.

"Tati, did you sing in the choir, too?" Angel leaned over me to ask.

"Girl, naw. I did intentional stuff like coming in at the wrong part of the song and singing with the soloist. They kicked me out," she laughed.

"I cussed too much to do anything in church," Tatum said.

"I believe you too, heathen," Angel laughed.

"I grew up in a church in Texas, but once we moved away, I didn't really go back," Leona said.

"It wasn't an every Sunday occurrence, but BG, Papa and I went."

The church service began and it was a complete production compared to how it used to be when I was a kid. They had cameras, dancers, a full band, lights, and screens everywhere. I was impressed.

Reverend Folsom walked up to the podium. As a kid, when I saw him at the podium that meant it was time for me to tune out. I never really followed what he was talking about, but all the adults seemed to agree with everything he said.

"Welcome to our first-time visitors and hello friends to our returning guests. I am so happy to be here this morning. As you all know, we are opening another location in Sable Falls. Some of you make that long drive here every weekend for church, and we appreciate it, but now you will have something closer."

The audience clapped and cheered.

"After an exhaustive and prayerful search, the Pastoral committee has selected a new minister and I would like to introduce him to you today. He is a native Texan, hailing from Houston, where he pastored a church for ten years. He is single with no children and a dynamic man of God. Please allow me to introduce you to Pastor Israel Lewis. The new pastor of Greater Hope in Love – Sable Falls. He will bring our sermon for today."

The audience stood and applauded as the new pastor walked to the podium.

"Thank you for the warm welcome. I was more than happy to accept the appointment here at GHL. I've admired Pastor Folsom and all the work he's done here in the area. I am excited to dig my heels into the community and get to work. Today, I want us to look at the story of Jarius' daughter in Mark chapter five. Jesus was in the midst of the people who had just heard about a miracle he'd performed, when a synagogue ruler named Jarius came to tell Jesus that his daughter was dying. Jarius asked Jesus to lay his hands on his daughter so that she could live. Jesus began to head in the direction of Jarius' daughter, but along the way, he stopped to heal a woman and talk about her faith.

I read this and thought about how Jarius must've felt. Like he'd made his way to Jesus and Jesus said, "Okay, I'm coming but give me a minute." You know how Black people use the word minute. It could mean anywhere from one literal minute to several days. Jarius was probably extremely frustrated.

As Jesus was taking his time to get to Jarius' daughter, word came that the girl had died. The messengers asked Jarius, why are you still bothering Jesus? She's dead now. See, Jarius knew what he'd already petitioned God for. Yet, when it didn't happen immediately, people around him said, 'Give up. It's not going to happen.'

Have you ever had a dream or a goal that seemed unattainable by your own strength? You told other people about your plan or goal, and those people spoke negatively when it didn't happen right away? That's what Jarius experienced.

Jesus still kept moving in the direction of Jarius' daughter even after the announcement that the girl was dead. Why? Because Jesus knew the power of death and life was in his tongue.

Jesus went into Jarius' house, where the people were acting a fool. Jesus said she's not dead. She's sleeping. The people had the nerve to talk about Jesus. Jesus said, 'Aye, all y'all that had something negative to say, get out.' That's the Pastor Iz version. Jesus only kept the people close to Him that believed in Him. Jesus took the hand of the seemingly life-less girl and told her to arise. Guess what she did? Got up!"

The audience clapped.

"What am I saying to you today? There are dreams in your life that seem like they have died. There are goals that you've tossed to the side because you had people around you who ridiculed your dream and told you it would never happen. They said, why keep working on that when you don't see anything coming from it. Move on. It's dead. I am here to tell you that it's not dead! It's sleeping. Today is the day for dream revitalization. Today, you remove the naysayers from the room and only keep those people close that believe in your dream. It can happen! It can happen for you! Look at your neighbor and say, 'Neighbor, it can happen for you!'"

The audience turned and repeated his words.

When Angel said it to me, I felt the words' impact. I immediately thought about my restaurant. I knew it could really happen for me.

"Then look at this – Look at this," Pastor Israel said, trying to speak over the shouts and cries of the congregation. "Look, then Jesus told them to feed the girl. Are you hearing me? Feed your dream! Don't let it die! It doesn't matter how long it takes; your dreams will become a reality! Don't give up. Don't stop! Don't throw in the towel. He that has begun a good work in you will continue to complete it. God has not forgotten or given up on you! You will succeed!"

By the time he finished with his message, the people in the church had screamed, shouted, ran laps around the church, passed out on the floor. It was mayhem.

It was cool, though. I felt like he was speaking directly to me. I knew I needed to pursue Ethos.

Reverend Folsom stood and invited my family to the front for the christening ceremony.

"I remember when Sister Northcott gave birth to the twins. My wife and I were at the hospital because the doctors were concerned that they may not make it. They did. I remember how much mischief these two got into in Sunday school and choir rehearsal. They were something else," he laughed.

I laughed because Tati and I stayed in trouble.

"Now, they are both successful, bright, and talented people who we are so very proud of."

The church clapped.

"I am so happy to see the next generation born into this family and all the support that this little person has. We know that life dealt him a hard blow immediately when he lost his mother two days after he was born. We are grateful to God for the help He's sent to ease the load. Today we want to give Maximus Andrew Northcott, Man as his family calls him, back to the Lord."

He went through the entire ceremony passing Man from me to all three of his godparents. My mother and all the women cried the whole ceremony while Man fumbled with the pages of the Bible the reverend was holding. He didn't want to let go of Kerry's necklace to come back to me. He pulled his hat off a couple times, but all in all, it was a beautiful ceremony.

. . .

*A*ngel

Momma Pearl had outdone herself with the reception after the christening. She rented out a venue that was a rehabbed barn. All the décor was blue and white. My MAN bars were front and center on a table filled with all different types of candy.

Momma Pearl and some of her church friends prepared so much food, and it was all delicious. A DJ played songs while everyone mingled, danced, drank, and ate.

"This turned out so nice," BG said.

We were sitting at the head table, watching everyone have a good time. Man was on my lap, knocked out. All the festivities had worn him out.

"She did a great job. The ceremony was nice too."

"It was. I'm glad I came," BG said.

"I'm so glad you're here. This wouldn't have been right without you. I'm a godmom now," I smiled.

"A smart, beautiful, and happy godmom. That's a great combination," BG said.

"Yes, it is."

"He's worn himself out," Xander said after sitting down next to me.

"Yeah, being the center of attention is hard work."

"Xander," Reverend Folsom said as he approached. "This is Pastor Lewis."

Xander stood to greet Pastor Lewis.

"Israel is fine," Pastor Lewis responded.

They shook hands.

"This is my lady, Angel, and her grandmother, Mrs. Saint Rose," Xander introduced.

"Grandmother?" Reverend Folsom responded. "As in your mother's mother?"

"I gave birth to her mother, and her mother gave birth to her. That makes me her grandmother," BG responded.

I was used to people not believing that BG was my grandmother. If she was flattered by the response, she never let it show.

"Well, nice to meet you, Mrs. Saint Rose."

"Same, Reverend," BG responded.

"Your message was right on time, Pastor Israel," BG said.

"Thank you," Pastor Israel replied with a smile that showed a slight dimple in his left cheek.

Pastor Israel was of average height with a caramel complexion. He wore his naturally curly hair full on the top but faded on the sides. His brandy colored eyes were somewhat hidden behind thick-rimmed glasses, giving him a distinguished look. He was handsome.

"I wanted to introduce you to Israel because he will be living in your neck of the woods," Reverend Folsom said.

"Welcome. If there is anything I can help you with, let me know," Xander said.

"I do have one dilemma. The realtor I contacted to help me find a house has gone MIA. I don't have the time or energy to deal with someone that doesn't know how to handle business. Would you happen to know one?" Israel said.

"As a matter of fact, I do," Xander responded and looked at me.

"I will go and grab her," I said and passed the baby to Xander.

I hadn't really seen Leona since church. I weeded through the people and finally laid eyes on her.

"Hey," I said after I located Leona trying to take another Man chocolate bar from the candy table.

"What! You scared me!" Leona said.

"That's because you're over here doing something you know you have no business doing. I haven't seen you since church. Come with me. I have a potential client for you."

We made our way back to the group.

"Pastor Israel Lewis, this is..."

"Lee?" Pastor Israel finished.

"Hi, Iz," Leona said.

I looked from Leona to Pastor Israel.

"You know each other?"

"We do," Leona said without taking her eyes off him.

"What a small world," Reverend Folsom said.

"Can I speak with you?" Pastor Israel said to Leona.

She nodded and he led her away.

"I was wondering if I could steal you, Angel?" Xander said.

"I'll take the baby," BG volunteered.

He passed Man to BG then took my hand in his.

I heard Reverend Folsom ask BG where she was from as we walked away.

We walked out the back door of the barn. The weather was perfect. The sun was setting in the distance, creating a beautiful mix of purple, lilac, red, and orange, causing me to have a bonbon idea. I stored the thought away and continued to walk with Xander.

He led me to a huge tree.

"Look," he said and pointed to a carving in the tree. "Me and Tati did this one time when we were supposed to be with the group for vacation bible school."

"The reverend said you two were terrible," I laughed.

"We were. I know everyone was glad we grew up. So, wait before I ask about the service, did you know Leona knew the new pastor?"

"No! I have no idea what that is about. I know Lee's family moved from Texas when she was a teenager. Maybe she knew him then? She didn't mention it. She was hiding after church. I will have to get to the bottom of that."

"What did you think of the service?"

"It was beautiful. I'm glad Momma Pearl suggested it and planned it. The pictures are going to be beautiful. I couldn't be happier with the result."

"Me either. I told Mom how well it all came together. I'm surprised she didn't incorporate some amusement park rides or ponies or something. I think Tati helped keep her in check. Anyway, I asked you out here because I wanted to give you this," he said and handed me a small box that was beautifully gift wrapped with a white bow on top.

"Xander." I smiled and sat on the bench under the tree.

After carefully removing the bow, I removed the box's top. Inside was a silver necklace with a beautiful solitaire diamond hanging from it.

"This is gorgeous!"

"Do you like it?" he asked.

"I love it. Put it on me," I ordered with a big smile on my face.

He removed the necklace from the box and placed it around my neck. I touched it then smiled.

"I got it to match your earrings," he said as he smiled at me.

"I love it, Xander. Thank you."

"You deserve it. I love you."

"I love you, too."

13

Angel

The weekend in St. Helane was refreshing, fun, and memorable. Spending some alone time with Xander was terrific. Hanging out with all the girls was so much fun. Maximus' christening ceremony and becoming his godmother was more than I could ever ask for.

"I'm going to have a hard time leaving this little fella behind when it's time for me to go back home," BG said.

"I know. I wish you didn't have to go back. I love having you here."

"I love being here, but you know I still have my practice in LA..." BG trailed off.

"What? Is everything okay?"

"Yes, yes, everything is fine. I've just been thinking a lot about being alone in the house and the ability to do telehealth..."

I sucked in some air.

"BG! You would move here?"

"I like it here," she replied as she shrugged. "I just didn't know how you would feel about having your grandmother in the same city."

"Are you kidding me! That would be amazing! I could have Leona look for some houses for you, and in the meantime, you could stay here.

I mean, I would have to ask Xander, but I don't think he would mind," I rattled off.

"No, I wouldn't impose. I would have to get everything settled in LA, and I wouldn't come until I had a place to live," BG said.

"Man, you hear that? My BG is moving to Sable Falls!"

"Da-da."

I froze and looked at BG.

"Did he just say da-da?"

"Da-da," Man repeated.

"Oh. My. Gawd!," I yelled, "He just repeated it. Did you hear it?"

"I heard it, too," BG said.

I grabbed my phone and called Xander.

"Hey, everything okay?" Xander said when he answered the phone.

"Babe, Maximus just said da-da."

"No way," Xander said.

"Yes, let me see if he will say again."

"Man, say da-da," I encouraged.

He was back to blowing his spit bubbles.

"Man, your daddy is on the phone. Can you say it one more time?" I pleaded. "He said it twice, didn't he BG?"

"He did," BG confirmed.

"Da-da!" Man said.

"There! Did you hear it?"

"I did!" Xander said.

"He's going to be saying full sentences in no time," BG smiled.

⠿⠿ ⠶⠄ ⠿⠿ ⠶⠄ ⠿⠿

"Hey babe, I'm glad you could come over," Leona greeted me as I pushed Maximus' stroller into her office.

I hadn't ever physically been in her office. I'd seen it over FaceTime and in pictures. She'd done a great job using various hues of pink and acrylic furniture to make it feel feminine and open.

"Have a seat." She pointed to one of the acrylic chairs in front of her desk.

She worked on removing Man's restraints to lift him from his stroller.

BAILEY WEST

After she had him securely in her arms and had kissed his cheeks at least ten times, she sat down behind her desk.

Man loved everyone, but he had a special place in his heart for Leona and Tatum.

After the conversation with BG about moving to Sable Falls, I'd sent Leona a text. I asked her to start looking for a place with possible office space for BG. She was as excited as I was.

"Let me clear all of this up before I get started."

"Wait, you have to tell me what's up with Pastor Israel," I said.

"I don't want to rehash the past. Just know that we were...friends and then we weren't. I didn't expect to see him at church and definitely didn't think he would be here in Sable."

"Are you going to help him find a house?"

"Yes, I guess. It's business, right?" She shrugged.

In all the years I'd known Leona, I'd never seen her unsure about anything. I could tell there was more to the Israel Lewis story, but I didn't press.

"Okay, when you are ready to talk about it, I will be here. You know I'm not going to force the issue. You are okay, though, right?"

"As good as I can be. Let's talk about BG."

"Okay."

"So, with BG, I have a few places that I'm looking at for her. One historic place with that old Victorian charm made me think of her because she's so classy. It has an addition that would be great for her business and it's in the city," Leona handed me a picture of the house.

"This is pretty. Would it work with her needing a few months to tie up everything in LA?"

"Girl, who are you talking to? I make magic happen all the time, but I don't want to limit her choices. I am going to find a few other properties for her to look at. That's not why I asked you here, though."

"What's up?"

"I met a client yesterday who is looking to move some property that I think would interest you," Leona said.

"I'm not looking to buy a house."

"It's commercial," she said and passed me a picture.

I inhaled sharply after looking at the picture.

172

"This is *Comrades* in Central Market. Chef Antonio is the Executive Chef and owner. He's been there for years. He's not selling this."

"According to the two-hour-long meeting I had with him at his restaurant yesterday, yes, he is. He wants to move to Florida or somewhere warm. He will keep his other location, but the one in Sable Falls will close. He said he won't sell it unless another restaurant moves in. That's when I thought of you," Leona said.

I looked at the picture again.

"Well, you but not you per se. I know that Xander has been putting out real estate feelers for a commercial property. I didn't tell Chef Antonio who you guys were, but I did say that if he could keep his move to himself, I knew of a potential buyer," Leona explained.

"Lee, that would be amazing! This is the best location in Central Market."

"I know which is why his asking price will be a little steep, but the clientele is already there. We could work with that girl from school with the great marketing company – what's her name?"

"Valerie?"

"Yeah, Valerie. She would knock the marketing out of the park for the restaurant. I mean, I'm sure Xander already has some people in mind, but I have a list of people that would love to work with a new, Black-owned fine dining restaurant here in Sable Falls," Leona said.

"Xander is at work, but I'm sure he would be very interested in hearing all the details."

"Okay, well, let me put a presentation together. I will go and get some pictures and talk about price and timeframe with the owner, so I can be prepared with all the answers to his questions," Leona said.

"Thank you for thinking of him, Lee."

"I was thinking about you. Xander was just lucky through association and his love for my friend," she replied with a wink.

*X*ander
Work picked up as soon as I arrived back after Maximus' christening. My mother did a fantastic job of celebrating but not going all out. She did warn me that his first birthday party was going to be epic,

so I might as well prepare myself. I was okay with that. I wouldn't expect anything less.

I was happy that BG was in town spending time with Angel because I'd been swamped with work. My hours fluctuated, and most nights, both she and Man would be asleep by the time I arrived home. Finding time in the evening to FaceTime with them was important, so I would usually stop whatever I was doing to say goodnight. The demand at work was only fueling my drive to get Ethos open. I needed time with Maximus and Angel. I'd been thinking a lot more about our future together and making her my wife.

Leona had given me a presentation on the *Comrades* property that was going up for sale soon. That location in Central Market would be perfect for Ethos. The price was hefty, but it would be worth every penny. I couldn't have chosen a better location. Leona said Chef Antonio was willing to wait on me and my financing. I made an appointment with my financial advisor to see what I needed to do to get the financing started.

"Bottom line, you need an investor. You have the capital that can be pulled from your portfolio, but you can't afford to do it with your son and the retirement plan you have set up. The business would need to be a smashing success immediately. Not saying that it won't, but we can never judge how a new business will do. So, my advice, find a partner or investor," Marcus, my financial advisor, said.

After sitting back in the chair and releasing a defeated breath, I said, "So, I can do it myself, but it wouldn't be wise?"

"Absolutely not. If it were just you and you had no plans to have a family or retire by sixty, then maybe. However, you've mentioned your son and your lady at least a dozen times. It sounds like you are about to settle down, maybe have more kids. You can't afford to play with your money like that," Marcus answered.

I ran my hand down my face. I didn't want an investor because I didn't want anyone telling me how to run Ethos or trying to infuse their ideas. Investors came with demands, and my Type A personality would probably clash with them and their demands.

"If I want to do this myself, then what do I need to do?" I asked.

"Make a lot more money," Marcus shrugged. "What's wrong with just finding an investor. They are everywhere, especially in this town with all the eateries. They would jump at the chance to work with you. You could draw up a proposal of a percentage buy-in and then negotiate the details. Here, something like this."

Marcus wrote some numbers on a piece of paper and handed it to me.

"I'll consider it," I said and stood to shake his hand.

"Xander, you can make this happen. Just be smart about it, okay?"

"I hear you."

"*H*ey, why are you out here in the dark?" Angel asked.

I'd been sitting in the backyard mulling over my conversation with Marcus. I was kicking myself because I should've started the restaurant when I'd initially had the idea. It could've been established by now and making money.

Thinking about using my entire portfolio to invest in a business that could fail was a terrible idea, but I kept running that scenario through my mind. I knew I shouldn't do it, but I wanted to.

"Just thinking," I answered.

Angel sat on my lap.

"BG and Man are sleep. They fell asleep on me while we were watching a movie. I didn't hear you come in. What's wrong?"

I picked up my cigar and took a puff. I leaned my head to the side and blew out the smoke.

"What does that taste like?" Angel asked.

"You've never had one?"

"Nope," she shook her head.

"Open," I put the cigar to her mouth. "Don't inhale it. Take a pull and then release the smoke."

I watched her wrap her lips around the cigar thinking about how good her lips felt wrapped around me.

"Now take a sip of this," I passed her my whiskey glass.

She took a sip and passed the glass back to me.

"You handled that well for the first time," I said.

"That's not your first time saying that," she winked.

175

She leaned in and kissed me, then pulled away.

"So, is this you? You have a problem, so you go and hide until you figure it out? You don't like to share?" she asked.

"Is it that bad?"

"If you are in a relationship, it's terrible."

I shrugged and took another sip of my drink.

"So, are you going to tell me what's wrong or do I have to pull it out of you?"

She looked at my crotch then back at me.

"I mean...either way could work," I replied with a lazy grin. "But I went to talk to my financial advisor today, and I didn't like what he had to say."

"What did he say?"

"He basically said I couldn't do it without an investor. After the meeting, he called me and told me he's set up a meeting with a potential investor. So, I guess I will take it."

"You wanted to do it without an investor, right?" Angel asked.

"Yeah, I don't want the headache of someone trying to manipulate my vision."

"It's a means to an end, baby. It won't be permanent. Remember that," she encouraged.

"I have plans for our future. I need Ethos to work so I can make my plans a reality."

"Well," she said as she straddled my lap. "You have the plan." She kissed my right cheek. "You have the drive and know-how." She kissed my left cheek. "You will make it happen," she said before kissing my lips.

She moved her hand to unbuckle my belt.

"BG is in the house," I said, but I wasn't stopping her.

"BG is asleep," she said and tugged on my trousers. I lifted my hips to assist her in pulling them down. "Man is asleep." She lifted her dress and sat back down on my lap.

"What happened to that sweet, innocent girl I first met?" I asked.

She moved her panties to the side and sank down on my hardness, "Your dick changed her life."

. . .

*X*ander

I went back and forth about taking the meeting with this investor Marcus had found for me. I didn't know their name, but he told me that they'd invested in startup businesses before. They were looking to get into the restaurant industry.

I chose my brown suit and blue shirt with light blue stripes. My brown tie and brown shoes finished the outfit.

"You look delicious," Angel said

"Thank you, baby. Maybe after tonight, I will have a better idea of which way to go with Ethos."

"I think you will," she said, smiling.

I arrived at the restaurant and was seated immediately. I informed the Maître D that my guest would be coming soon.

After ordering a glass of whiskey, I heard a familiar voice.

"Wow, look at this?" Emmaline said. "I didn't know you knew Marcus."

"What are you talking about?" I asked, instantly irritated by her presence.

"My father is looking to invest in a restaurant and Marcus told him about a young, Black chef that was looking to open a spot here. I wouldn't have guessed it was you," she said.

I couldn't believe my luck. Was the investor Marcus connected me with really Emmaline's father?

She sat down across from me and the waitress immediately handed her a menu.

"Thank you," she said to the waitress. "I will take a glass of Cabernet immediately, please."

"I don't know why you are ordering a drink. This won't work, Emma."

I sent a text to Marcus.

Xander: You connected me with Larry Stonefield?
Marcus: Yes. He was looking for an investment opportunity.

Xander: Don't ever connect me with anyone without telling me who they are first. This was a terrible idea.

Marcus: Sorry. Would you like me to find someone else?

Xander: HELL NO!

I tucked my phone back in my pocket in preparation to leave.

"You've been talking about this little idea of yours for years. You've come this far. You might as well tell me what your plans are. Father will want me to report back something."

"You can tell him that it was me and I said no thank you," I responded.

"Xander, don't be like that. You broke up with me, remember? I'm not bitter or angry. Business is business, right? Let's just talk about that. Daddy is willing to offer a fifty-five percent buy-in to your restaurant. In return, he would want some creative input and access to all the financials. He would also reserve the right to hold on as an investor for five years. No talk of buy out until the five years have passed," Emmaline said.

"No," I responded.

"No? This is where we negotiate," Emmaline said.

"There is no negotiation. I don't want to work with you or your father. I will figure this restaurant out on my own."

"You were always that type—all bullheaded and introspective. Always tried to figure things out on your own. You never asked me for help."

"I didn't need your help. Besides, you interjected your help all over the place. That was part of our problem."

"Maybe if you would've talked more, I wouldn't have felt the need to insert myself," she countered.

"I didn't come here to rehash the past. That's over," I said.

"It couldn't have been all bad, right, Xan?" Emmaline asked and reached to touch my hand.

I retracted it before she could.

"Oh, it's the nanny...huh?" she turned up her nose.

"Even if I wasn't in a healthy, thriving relationship, this – *us* – would never be a thing ever again. Thank you for your consideration, but I will find my own financing."

After swallowing down the rest of my drink, I stood and placed enough money on the table for our drinks plus a tip.

"You will be back. You won't find anyone in this town that will finance a startup restaurant with a chef that hasn't been in the kitchen in years," Emmaline said.

"I'll never be back. Have a great life," I said as I walked away.

I drove around town, trying to clear my head after that conversation with Emmaline. Her words kept playing in my head, "You won't find anyone in this town that will finance a startup restaurant with a chef that hasn't been in the kitchen in years."

I was irritated with myself for even entertaining her conversation for any length of time. I was frustrated that I let Marcus set me up without asking more questions. I wasn't any further along than I had been when I'd first picked up my business plan again.

"Hey," I said after entering the house and finding Angel sitting in the living room listening to music.

"Hey, how was the meeting?" she asked.

"It was a meeting." I shrugged and continued to the back of the house.

She followed me into my bedroom.

"So, give me details."

"I mean, it was unproductive. I don't know which way I want to go with this. I'm going to hop in the shower real quick."

I hadn't made eye contact with her until after I announced my shower. Something was in her eyes, but I couldn't pinpoint what it was.

"Okay." She shrugged. "You can finish telling me about it when you're done with your shower."

"I mean, it's not really much to tell, Angel," I responded.

"Humph," she said. "So, you're finished telling me about it then?"

"Yes. That's what it's not really much to tell means," I snapped.

Her neck jerked like she'd been slapped. Her nostrils flared as she squinted at me. After swiping on her phone, she held it to my face.

"This was in my DMs," she said.

There was a picture of me on Instagram, sitting across the table from Emmaline. The caption read:

> Why only show his arm when I can show his whole face.
> He knew she was a peasant when he got with her.
> #screenshotthis #theyalwayscomeback
> #doublebacknever #norepeats #crownme

I looked at the picture then looked at Angel. I had no idea Emmaline had taken a picture of me and posted it on her social media. That look in Angel's eyes was anger. I'd never seen her angry.

"You weren't going to tell me that your meeting was with Emmaline?"

Angel tilted her head and waited for me to respond. I was at a loss for words. I didn't know how to reply.

"That's you, right? At a restaurant with Emmaline, right?" Angel asked.

"I mean..."

"If you say 'I mean' one more time. That's your tell. Did you know that? You preface a sentence with 'I mean' when you are about to hold something back. Say it again, Xander," Angel fumed.

"I didn't know that I was meeting with her. Marcus didn't tell me who it was," I explained.

"And what? You didn't recognize her when she sat down at the table across from you?"

"I did, but..."

"Great way to break your first promise to always tell me the truth and never keep anything from me," Angel said.

"Nothing happened! I didn't even stay at dinner with her."

"And you couldn't have said that when I asked? Do I always need proof of you doing some shady looking crap to get a clear answer from you?"

"No, Angel, I should've told you she was there," I answered.

"I couldn't care less about who you have dinner with, Xander. Even though she was the chick you were with before me, I'm not jealous or insecure. I'm confident enough in what we have for that not to be an issue. I don't even care about her petty ass post that she sent to my DMs. You came back here. My problem is that I asked you and you didn't say *anything*. And then had the nerve to try to get a lil' attitude when I asked you twice," Angel said, holding up two fingers.

"It's her father's company and..."

"Oh, I don't want to hear it now. Keep that crap to yourself like you do everything else," she said and walked away.

"Angel, don't..." I rushed out.

She closed the door behind her.

After changing out of my suit, I took a shower giving me some time to think and Angel some time to calm down. *Why do I keep to myself instead of sharing what I'm feeling?* I thought. Apparently, I did it a lot because both Angel and Emmaline had mentioned it. I didn't want to upset Angel and I definitely didn't want to lose her.

I tapped on Angel's bedroom door before entering. She was lying down with her back to the door.

I pulled the covers back and got in the bed with her. I sat with my back against the headboard. She didn't acknowledge my presence. Trying to figure out where to begin, we sat in silence until I finally spoke.

"Baby, I'm sorry. It's just that this business is all that I can think about. I want it to succeed so bad. I wasn't trying to keep anything from you. I promise I wasn't. I think I've been alone in my thoughts and plans for so long that it's hard to share them. I used to have all these big, bold goals and dreams. I would share them with people and ultimately get talked out of them. I just decided to keep my plans and thoughts to myself until I had them all figured out."

"I've only encouraged your dreams," Angel said with her back still towards me.

"Yes, you have, and I'm sorry for treating you like the people who didn't. I was also a little embarrassed the meeting didn't work out," I admitted.

"Why would you be embarrassed?" she turned around and asked.

"Because." I shrugged. "I'm trying to build something for us. For our family and I don't know how to get it done. When I talked to BG, she asked what I could bring to the table. I want to give you the world, Angel. You and Maximus. I don't know how to do that and it's driving me crazy," I admitted.

"I didn't ask you for the world, Xander. All I asked for is loyalty, respect, love, and communication. The same way you told me you wanted me to talk and share with you is the same way I want you to share with me. If I'm not your nanny but truly your girl and friend, then tell me what's going on. Don't force me to ask."

"I hear you and I'm sorry. For the record, nothing happened with Emmaline."

"I'm not concerned about her. It's like people with money versus people without. People who don't have money are always talking about what they have. People with money never talk about it. Same with me and Emmaline. I don't have to brag about what's mine," Angel finished with a shrug.

I smiled. I loved Angel and her confidence.

"So, tell me about the meeting with Marcus and then tell me about the meeting with Emmaline."

I told her about both meetings, not leaving out anything, including Emmaline trying to touch my hand.

"So, you would need an investor to come to the table with at least sixty-percent of what you need for you to move forward?"

"Yes," I answered.

"What about a partner instead of an investor? Someone who could bring the money to the table but not have to be paid back because they own the business, too?" she asked.

"I am such a type A cook. I don't think I would work well with anyone in the kitchen except for you."

"Then ask me," she said.

"Huh?"

"You don't want me to be your partner?"

"Hell yeah, I want you to be my partner. I didn't ask you because I didn't want you to feel pressured to get back in the kitchen. Eventually, if you expressed interest, I wanted to loop you in."

"I want to be wherever you are, Xander. I only have one stipulation."

"Anything," I quickly responded.

"I want to get the small space next to the restaurant to open Midnight by Ethos. I want to only open it on Friday evenings, Saturdays and Sundays for brunch. That's where I will premiere all my new chocolate creations and have live music," she said.

"Absolutely! Now, all we need to do is find someone to put up the money and we are good."

"I've taken care of that. That's why I was so eager to find out about your meeting. I wanted to tell you what happened."

"What happened?"

"While you were out, BG got a call informing her that Papa's estate funds have been released. He left her a substantial amount so she can move down earlier than she anticipated. He also left me enough to bring my money to the table for our partnership. And BG wants to be a silent partner, so she will put up a percentage as well. If that's okay with you."

"That's more than okay. That's amazing."

The End

EPILOGUE

Xander

EPILOGUE

*X*ander

"Aye, quiet down. Pastor Israel is going to say a prayer before we open these doors. Pastor."

"I am honored to be the one to bless this establishment. Xander and I are more recent friends, but he and his family have quickly become my family. I appreciate this opportunity," Israel said.

Israel had quickly become part of our family. He hadn't permanently moved to Sable yet, but he was here every weekend preaching at his church. Angel and I had become members of the church and had found Israel to be a great source of sound counsel and friendship.

We still weren't sure about the origins of he and Leona's relationship. Neither shared much of the story except they grew up together. They were cordial when we were all around each other, but you could tell something was going on.

"We thank you, Yahweh God, for this blessing that you've bestowed on my family, Xander and Angel. When those people pour into those doors, we pray that they will feel the love between the owners and the love the staff has put into the food. Let them spread the word that Ethos is the place to eat. We pray a triple fold blessing over everyone under the sound of my voice. Now unto Him that can do exceedingly, abundantly, above all that we can ask or think. To Him be glory and honor, dominion, and power forever and ever. Amen," Israel prayed.

"Amen!" the staff cheered.

"Thanks, bro," I said after hugging Israel, "Alright, today is the day. We've had five test runs and learned something each time. Let's put all that knowledge to work tonight. Everyone knows where they are supposed to be and what they are supposed to do. Stay in your lane! Angel and I are so happy that you are our staff. We appreciate the long hours, the sacrifice, the moods, and everything that came along with it, but now we are here."

"Yes," Angel said, "I couldn't be prouder of each and every one of you. Thank you for taking on this task with us. We will work hard when those doors open, but when they close, we will celebrate! Y'all ready?"

The staff yelled various affirmations.

After months of renovations, training, and planning, Ethos was finally opening. We purchased the old *Comrades* for less than the owned had originally planned on selling it for because he'd heard of Angel. The caveat of the agreement to sell it for less was that Angel would do a guest spot at his restaurant in Florida to which she immediately agreed.

All the plans I had written down from the various sections to the color schemes were followed to perfection. Garrett had agreed to be our supplier for our farm to table menu and he provided us with his seasonal rum.

Midnight by Ethos was set to open the following weekend. As Angel had asked, it would only be open Friday nights, Saturdays and Sundays for brunch. The warm chocolate and gold décor of Midnight made you feel like you were inside a chocolate confection. She'd designed so many new chocolate treats and was excited to debut them.

Between BG and my mom, we never needed a babysitter for Man. Mom came up often and BG had moved about fifteen minutes away from Angel and me.

Everyone was present for the grand opening; even Angel's mother Lydia came. She was set to sing with a band for the grand opening of Midnight.

"Xander, Maximus, and I are going to go and greet the customers, then we will be back to work. Chef Perry, Chef Daryl, and Chef Herbert will oversee their respective areas. We all know what we are doing. Let's make this an experience they'll never forget!" Angel said.

Everyone cheered.

We worked hard and stayed busy the entire night. The staff was terrific. The food was not only good, but it was beautiful. Our grand opening went perfectly.

"Are you tired?" I asked Angel while I rubbed her feet.

Man was sleeping in his favorite position, with his face right in the middle of Angel's breasts.

"I'm tired, but I'm so satisfied. Today was amazing. It can only get better," Angel said.

I pulled a small box out of my pocket.

"I got you something," I said and handed her the box.

"What is it?"

"You have to open it and find out. Wait, before you open it. Let me put Man in his bed."

I pried Man from her and took him to his room.

After returning, I said, "Okay, open it."

She quickly snatched the bow off the top and opened it.

She sucked in air.

"Xander..." she looked at me.

"I'd been trying to find the right time all evening to ask you. I wanted to do it in front of the staff. Then I wanted to do it in front of the customers. Then I decided, I wanted you all to myself when I asked. So, Miss Angelica Saint Rose, will you be my wife?"

"Of course, yes!" she replied with a tearful smile.

I pulled the chocolate diamond solitaire from the box and placed it on her finger.

"Loving you and loving man were the best decisions I'd made in my life."

THANK YOU!

I asked my Facebook group Bailey's Coterie to help me name these characters. They came through in grand fashion.

Xander was named by Keica Smart

Jacory was named by Joslyn Marks

Maximus was named by Angie Rodriguez

Sable Falls was named with a lot of help from Marlee Rae

Thank you ladies.

Thank you to all the Indie supporters who wait patiently (and sometimes not so patiently) for our books to drop. I appreciate you more than words can ever express.

To my Heavenly Father, I once again publicly acknowledge the ongoing private relationship we have. You are my everything. Thank you for your love, your gifts, and your Spirit that lives in me.

Thank you for the ability, space, focus and time to create because
I AM MOST LIKE YOU WHEN I AM CREATING

Ian Noble appeared courtesy of Te' Russ. Ian's story can be found in the Noble Love series.

Kingston Wright appeared courtesy of Danielle Allen. Kingston's story can be found in Truth or Dare

Also by

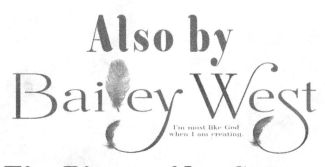

I'm most like God
when I am creating.

The Bluette Men Series

Blue's Beauty
Ezekiel's Passion
Paxton's Peace

The Valentine Law Series

Serving Time
Free Indeed
Trusting the Process
Depth of Love

Lessons In Love Series

Iuu Love

LET'S KEEP IN TOUCH

Bailey-West.com - My Website

Bailey's Coterie - My Facebook Group

Subscribe to my newsletter

CPSIA information can be obtained
at www.ICGtesting.com
Printed in the USA
LVHW030848271220
675096LV00006B/975

9 798551 645443